ZARAQUEL
MORAL COMPASS

A BLOOD PROPHECY NOVELLA

Barb Jones

This is a work of fiction. Names, characters, places, and incidents are products of the author's imagination or are used fictitiously and are not to be construed as real. Any resemblance to actual events, locations, organizations, or persons, living or dead, is entirely coincidental.

World Castle Publishing, LLC
Pensacola, Florida
Copyright © Barb Jones 2022
Paperback ISBN: 9781958336397
eBook ISBN: 9781958336403
First Edition World Castle Publishing, LLC, July 18, 2022
http://www.worldcastlepublishing.com

Licensing Notes

Cover: Steven J. Catizone
Editor: Maxine Bringenberg

To Arianna and Kaiden – Always written for you and because of you!

Author's Note

Welcome to the world of Blood Prophecy! I get a lot of questions about how these novellas should be read in conjunction with the novels. Here is my suggested list:

Queen's Destiny
Novella: Amber
Queen's Enemy
Novellas Chloe and Marcus
Queen's Ascension
Novella: Machiel
Novella: Zaraquel
Rise of the Hunter (coming soon)

Of course, you can read the novellas (Amber, Chloe and Marcus) after either *Queen's Destiny* or *Queen's Enemy*. However, I suggest that Machiel and Zaraquel be read after the third installment, *Queen's Ascension*, and in that order. Why? Because Machiel and Zaraquel are written to help introduce you to Book 4: *Rise of the Hunter*, which is right after the third novel.

I wrote this novella to bring Zaraquel out more as the avenging angel as her role in the prophecy reached a turning point in her young life. Not quite an adult, but not a child either, she needs to forge her own path, which raises questions on her morality. And, of course, I leave my readers wanting more—so stay tuned for the next novel! As always, thank you for supporting me. I am very humbled to bring the world of

Blood Prophecy to you.

CHAPTER 1

Zaraquel

Months had passed since Rae's sacrifice. Day in and day out, Zaraquel spent her time near Rae's commemorative statue. It was lifelike, a replica of Rae; even the slight smirk was done to perfection. Zaraquel sat there often and so still that when others passed by, they thought she, too, was a statue. Sometimes she made them scream when she made the slightest movement.

She wasn't dead, but she shouldn't be alive either.

A little bit of her had died the moment Rae sacrificed herself. Zaraquel missed her so much that losing Rae felt like she lost a limb or a piece of her. When she lost Rae, it was like she lost an essential part of herself. A large part of her identity. A part of her soul.

On one of her many walks around the perimeter of The Order, Zaraquel was bombarded with thoughts that consumed her.

Summer's over, and I'll be starting high school without *Rae.*

There must be some way to get her back — a magical way? Maybe. Ugh, I don't know.

I wonder where Loquiel is.

Her heart was split in two — one half for Rae and the other for Loquiel.

The worst thing about her broken heart was that she no longer had her best friend to tell everything to. Not that Rae knew about Loquiel, but Zaraquel missed the chance that she would share the news with her. When she hadn't thought about Rae, she thought about Loquiel.

Her first love and first heartbreak. To her, it wasn't a childhood love. She was a young woman. And Loquiel was a young man. Young people in love.

He broke her heart. He broke *her.* Loquiel betrayed her by working with the Tall Dark Man. He said it was *for* her, that he loved her too much. He just wanted to make her love him. Didn't he know that in their mindspeak, in the meeting of their lips, in the way they spent all night talking…didn't he know he didn't need a spell for that? She was already in love with him.

He was just too stupid to see it. Maybe they were both stupid for missing the signs. She was no longer a child in how she felt. Now she'd never know.

As she made the trek back, she paused at the scene before her eyes. Her parents walked hand in hand as they took their daily afternoon stroll. Zaraquel saw it in their eyes since the battle; they seemed lighter, happier. Her mother dipped her head back as she laughed, while her father smirked knowingly. Her father was always on her side, but every time she tried to speak to him, he was never sure what he could say or do. She was glad they were happy, but it didn't mean their joy didn't sting. She was bitter, colder even. Zaraquel was brave enough to admit it. She knew this would affect her role as avenging angel and her morality, but she didn't care anymore.

She turned away to alleviate the ache, but she saw another happy couple—Auntie Amber and Malakai—gathered in each other's arms. With Malakai's back against a tree and legs open wide, Auntie Amber sat nestled in between and in his arms. She read aloud as he played with the ends of her hair. Her thoughts hardened.

Perfect, just perfect. Everyone is living the dream. Everyone but me.

They didn't see the hurt in her eyes or hear the tears she cried in the shower. Zaraquel hid it too well; she didn't want them to know she was hurting and in agony. She was a warrior angel, part of the prophecy, and therefore, she was not weak.

Her mantra since the aftermath: I AM NOT WEAK.

She flew up to her room before they could see her facade slip. Zaraquel paced around the room she once shared with her best friend. Everything was as Rae left it—her bed, her shoes on the floor, her magic books. It was as if she never passed, at least within the walls of their room. However, Zaraquel knew very well that one day her stuff would just be a distant memory.

Zaraquel landed on her bed with a huff, lying flat on her back. She searched the crevices of her mind for possible solutions. As if the memories hit her on rewind, she saw it all as if it were a movie.

She remembered all the fun times she shared with Rae, the laughter, the practical jokes. Zaraquel remembered all their preparation, the training, and the spellcasting, all in the name of the battle. Things were supposed to be fine and dandy after they won; instead, there were great casualties that affected them all, even though it appeared that Zaraquel was the only one suffering. So many were lost in the battle despite the numbers that survived. Zaraquel was saddened with the losses. The battle kept playing on a loop; it was the nightmare that kept her up most nights.

The battle.

Why didn't she think of it before?

Of course! she thought to herself. She knew that Amber's resurrection was a one-time thing, given that it was written in the prophecy. But could there be an exception? Why not? She was the avenging angel, a prominent force in the prophecy.

As she wanted to save her heart and mind, Zaraquel rushed out of her room and down the stairs right into what used to be Merlin's office. Well, it now belonged to Uncle Mac, but that was beside the point since he was out recruiting new members for the Order—whether they were teachers or students, she didn't know. She didn't really pay much attention. Zaraquel was too busy drowning in her grief.

Nevertheless, she snuck into his office in search of the forbidden magic books. She opened drawers and looked through his extensive library, but to no avail. An hour passed by, and nothing. Frustrated, she sat on the floor and leaned back against one of the walls, her head hitting the wood with a thud.

Zaraquel stopped, "Was that — ?"

She hit her head against the wall once more — a thud. It was hollow. She turned and propped herself up on her knees. There was a separation between the wall and the floor. She looked at the rest of the floorboards, but that tiny sliver of black was nowhere to be seen.

Out of curiosity, Zaraquel placed her finger beside the gap. She felt it — the air that ran out of that crevice and onto the pad of her finger.

"This must be it!" she whispered excitedly. "*Patentibus.*" She chanted over and over until the door slowly opened. With cautious steps, she entered.

The room was dark and oddly cold for being insulated into the wall. She unfurled her wings, wrapping them around her to keep herself warm.

"*Ignis.*" A little ball of fire appeared out of thin air and floated above her palm. She sighed at feeling the sudden warmth. However, she was on a mission: the books. The fire showed her the way into the room, which she noticed was not a room at all, but a tunnel.

As she walked deeper into the tunnel, the colder it got. And there they were — encased in the wall was the set of books with forbidden magic. With a flick of her fingers, she sent the little fireball flying, and it floated before her. As she gathered the books in her hands, she felt a sudden rush of power, as if she were being electrocuted. It didn't hurt—in fact, she felt better.

The pain and the ache were gone. *She* was better.

"How could that be? I didn't even say a spell." The longer she held the books, she began to sense there was something compelling her to continue down the path. It was a woman's voice that whispered, though she couldn't quite make it out. The whispers slithered into her ear. She walked further down the tunnel and was met with a large, solid door. She felt the door to see if she could sense what was behind it, but she couldn't.

She placed her ear beside the door, and the woman's whispers grew louder. Zaraquel had never heard her voice, yet here and now, she was all that Zaraquel could hear. One hand held the books while the other made its slow descent to the doorknob.

The metal of the doorknob was equally as cold as the tips of her fingers reaching for it. She didn't turn the knob because someone called out to her.

"Zaraquel? Where are you, honey?" Her father yelled from somewhere in the house, and she yanked her hand away before she could see what was on the other side.

"Shit," she quickly whispered. "Ad cubiculum." The books were transported out of her hands and into a hidden compartment in her room that she and Rae had made to hold all their secrets and precious trinkets.

Her wings opened as she prepared to take flight. With one last look at the door, Zaraquel promised herself she would return to unlock the mystery.

As if sensing that Zaraquel was up to something, her parents and Auntie Amber, sometimes Malakai, kept her company the ENTIRE weekend. They ate dinner together, watched a movie together. They were always together. Under any other circumstances, she would've enjoyed the company, but not now. She didn't have time to crack open the books or go back to the tunnel to finally open the door. She itched to go back down there. Zaraquel felt like she had to. She couldn't explain it. It felt like an impulse, like she *needed* to go there.

Nevertheless, her mother and Auntie Amber spent Saturday night with her picking out clothes for the new school year. Zaraquel waited for the mall to close soon. As Zaraquel looked through the racks of shirts and jeans, her mother showed her different options, some skirts and flowy shirts.

"How 'bout this one, sweetie?" It was a bright pink blouse with puffy sleeves.

Zaraquel's eyes bugged out in surprise, "Mom, c'mon! Really?"

"What? I thought it was cute." Her mother turned to Amber. "It's cute, right, Amber?"

Auntie Amber turned, and always the supportive friend, she agreed. "Chloe, *I* would wear that."

Zaraquel murmured, "That's the problem."

"Hey, I heard that!" Auntie Amber replied.

Meanwhile, her mother gave her a pointed look and pulled her aside. She cocooned her with her arm around her shoulder. Normally Zaraquel would feel safe, but that day she was simply annoyed. She tried to shrug her off, but her mother pulled her in closer.

"Hey, Z?" Zaraquel didn't respond, nor did she look at her. "Zaraquel," her mother said more sternly.

Zaraquel finally looked up, and that's when Zaraquel knew Chloe could see it—the pain, the hurt. She quickly turned away.

Her mother's face softened as she held Zaraquel's chin up with her finger. "We were just trying to help, y'know? Bring a little color into your life."

Zaraquel gestured to her all-black and darkly colored attire in the bag, "I'm fine with this."

"It's not wrong to be happy. Even if just a little bit."

"Mom, she was my best friend."

Her mother pulled her into a tight hug, "I know, baby. I know."

***

The next night, Amber volunteered to take her school supply shopping. She bounced up and down the aisles placing items in the cart as she went. Her aunt was a ball of energy.

Zaraquel looked up at Malakai and sighed. "Is she always like this?"

"Around stationery and supplies, yes." She saw him quirk a smile as he looked lovingly at her aunt. They walked in silence as she continued to look at the store's vast array of pens lined up against the wall.

"Ah, to be in school again," Auntie Amber remarked dreamily. At this, both Zaraquel and Malakai shared a chuckle.

Auntie Amber whipped around at the sound of the laughter and sneered. "I'm onto the two of you."

Zaraquel noticed that Malakai shook his head and

smiled at Auntie Amber's antics. Amber continued on her merry way, apparently ignoring them, which was fine with her. Side by side in comfortable silence, Zaraquel and Malakai followed Auntie Amber's every twist and turn as she went through the aisles.

"It gets easier," Malakai stated out of the blue.

Zaraquel looked up at him, a bit confused. "Hmm?"

"Losing someone."

She stopped, frozen in her place. Had she not been hiding her feelings as well as she thought?

I have to step it up, she thought to herself.

He gently grabbed her by the shoulders, and she could feel the warmth radiating off him and onto her. He held her as if he knew she would run away. Malakai went down on one knee, so they were at eye level.

"It gets easier over time," he continued. "That doesn't mean it stops hurting. It will always hurt. The pain of losing her just gets a little easier to deal with. Rae may not physically be here, but she's always in here."

He placed a hand over his heart and then pointed to hers. Zaraquel struggled not to cry, but she couldn't keep the tears from falling. She clutched onto him and buried her face in his arms.

"Thanks, Mal." Her voice sounded small, even to her.

CHAPTER 2

Zaraquel

That night she went over her weekend in her head. Although she was afraid to admit it, she was tired of being sad. What more could she take? She was heartbroken in more ways than one. She turned to look at Rae's bed, and Zaraquel was hit with a memory not long before the battle.

Three Nights Before the Battle

Rae and Zaraquel sat in their respective beds and talked till they fell asleep, as was their usual. Rae was beginning to doze off when Zaraquel threw a pillow in her face.

She sat up straight. "Hey, Z! What the heck?"

Zaraquel giggled and responded, "I can't sleep."

"And that means I shouldn't either?" Rae threw the pillow back, only to have Zaraquel dodge it in return.

Zaraquel bit her bottom lip, her nerves beginning to

show. She noticed that Rae stopped and immediately hopped onto her bed. "Z? What's up?"

"The heavens," Zaraquel quipped back.

Rae wrapped her arm around her. "I'm serious."

"I know," Zaraquel responded with a touch of sadness and worry in her voice. "It's just that I don't know. I...I have this feeling that something's gonna go badly with this battle."

"C'mon, Z, that's just the nerves talking. You're an angel with a vampire and a witch for parents—you got this," Rae said confidently.

Zaraquel hugged her tightly and whispered, "I have you too, Rae."

"We have each other," Rae smiled.

The two laughed as they crashed down on Zaraquel's bed, facing the ceiling.

"I still can't sleep," Zaraquel admitted with a laugh.

"Really? Ugh, okay." Rae was silent for a couple of seconds, and with a wave of a hand, the ceiling was made translucent. The stars and the moon hung brightly in the sky. It brought a smile to Zaraquel's face.

"Wow, that's amazing."

"I know. And Z?"

"Hmm?"

"Go to sleep."

Zaraquel smiled at Rae's brisk humor. Moments later, the girls, who acted more like sisters, fell asleep beside each other.

***

Present Day

Zaraquel looked up and expected to see the stars, but the spell had withered away just as Rae did. Nevertheless, she forced her tired eyes to close and soon fell into a deep slumber. When she dreamt—and not of the nightmare that often played in her head—she dreamt of Rae and sometimes Loquiel, but oftentimes it was Rae. Zaraquel concocted what she wanted in her dreamworld. No monsters that killed or wars or blood prophecies. Her dream world was as she desired.

Tonight was no different than any other night. Outside the ice cream shop, she patiently waited for Rae. Seconds later, there she was. This time, however, her skin took on a kind of shine. She glittered as the sun rays hit her.

Maybe she thought about it and manifested it into existence. Shrugged it off and gladly took the ice cream cone that Rae offered.

She licked it. "Mmmm, so good."

Rae rolled her eyes and bumped her shoulder. "I know. That's why I got it."

They inhaled the creamy deliciousness and tossed their napkins in the trash. They stood to continue their fun day in the park.

"So, I know what you're trying to do, Z."

She flipped her hair over her shoulder, trying to shield her eyes from her best friend. "I have no idea what you're talking about." She walked ahead, and Rae grabbed her shoulder, forcing her to stop.

"Don't do it. It's too dangerous."

"You can't tell me what to do, Rae! You're dead!" Her lips quivered from the tears that fell. "You don't know how hard it is, being here…without you."

Rae pulled her into a tight embrace. "I'm sorry," she whispered. "But you have to stop—bad things will happen if you continue."

Zaraquel dislodged from the hug and looked at her as if Rae had grown a second head. "Why are you saying this? Don't you want to come back? Don't you miss me?" Her voice broke.

Rae looked at her with tears brimming her eyes. "God, I miss you so much, you don't even know. Look under the floorboard. The answer starts there." Her voice was hoarse with what Zaraquel took for sadness, but it sounded deeper somehow. Zaraquel quirked her head to the side.

"Rae?"

Rae waved a hand over her, and Zaraquel fell into a dreamless rest. She floated off into the clouds as Rae watched her go.

***

Loquiel

He knew Zaraquel didn't want to see him, but he couldn't help himself from checking in on her from time to time, especially after the loss of Rae. As he hovered above her bed, he saw the tears escape from her eyes. He wanted to wipe the sadness from her face, but he didn't. Loquiel chose not to risk it if he touched her and she woke up.

It was wrong going into her head like that when she was the most vulnerable, but he didn't know any other way to get through to her. He magically disguised himself as Rae and hoped that his message stayed with her and she listened. He knew she sought a way to bring Rae back, but it would destroy her if she succeeded.

The path that she was on was far too dangerous. Not only did she risk death, but the purity of her soul was also at risk. Zaraquel had managed to live up to her prophecy and saved the world from destruction, but who was going to save her?

He made it his mission to help and save her heart and soul. No matter the cost, Zaraquel was his priority, despite his guilt. He cloaked himself, and no magical being—good or bad—would be able to notice his presence. Loquiel lived by his duty, an invisible angel.

Loquiel remembered the fight he had with the Tall Dark Man for failing the task he was given. He was only to watch and report. As he got to know Zaraquel and how much she had grown into a strong young woman, he fell in love. This was against his orders, but he didn't care. Loquiel was a young demon, a fallen angel, as well. He believed in the lies The Tall Dark Man told him, including how Zaraquel would turn against her family, and yet she didn't. The memories of his feelings towards her brought a smile to his face.

As the sun rose, he faded away before Zaraquel could sense him. With his broken heart, he watched over her as he promised her once before. Not even the Tall Dark Man knew what he did.

***

Zaraquel

Despite the fact that she woke up with the dreaded feeling she shouldn't proceed with her plan of saving Rae, she rose from her bed with renewed energy to forge on. She glanced at her clock — it was five in the morning. Zaraquel was not tired one bit, which was unusual given the last few months. With a yawn and a long stretch, she swung her feet over the mattress and plopped down in the space between her bed and Rae's.

There was nothing. It was empty.

She closed her eyes and repeated as Rae had taught her, "*Videtur.*"

She cracked open one eye, and then the other, and Zaraquel's lips erupted into a smile. There before her was a small chest, rectangular with a domed top. Teal and rusted with patina, it was heavy, but Zaraquel was strong enough to open it. Inside were the books from the tunnels. She dug them out, expecting to find something else. Semi-disappointed, she closed the lid and took some supplies from under her bed for research.

A loud rumble of her stomach interrupted Zaraquel's line of thinking. She clicked on her phone to reveal that three hours had passed.

"Shit."

Zaraquel, on her stomach, turned to lie on her back. She was surrounded by all the books propped open. Several pages from each book were marked with tiny tabs. There was one constant symbol on these books — the pentacle. It was similar to the pentagram, but the pentacle was used for dark magic. Zaraquel wondered about some of the other symbols, so she kept reading and writing it all down. Her notebook was full of doodles and notes, ingredients for spells—the works. As she looked at some of the notes, she'd taken and the pictures in the books, she grew more confident that this would be the way to bring her back. Rae. She missed Rae so much.

Unbeknownst to Zaraquel, the air in her room crackled with energy.

She rubbed her eyes, and her stomach growled loudly once more. She looked down. "Shut up. I heard you already. Jesus," she said, exasperated.

Zaraquel walked out of her room, through the communal living area, and into the kitchen, eager to munch on some breakfast. On the fridge was a note from her mom that read, *Dad and I went to the coven for a bit. Be back soon! P.S. Auntie Amber is with Malakai if you need anything! XOXO, Mom.*

Zaraquel smiled at the perfect cursive on pink paper. "This is perfect," she said to herself.

She poured herself some cereal in a bowl, followed by milk. Excitedly she hurried into Uncle Mac's study and opened the false wall. She trotted down the tunnel as she munched on her breakfast.

"I finally get to see what's behind that door!"

She heard the voice once more, and her legs moved faster of their own volition. She dropped her breakfast.

"Damn it."

The speed was ungodly. Zaraquel couldn't stop if she tried. Her hair swished past as if she were on a rollercoaster ride. Unfortunately, she had nothing to hold on to. With a loud thump, she stopped right in front of the door.

She touched the knob, and her finger was shocked. "Whoa."

She took the doorknob firmly in hand and twisted, and with a loud click, the door opened. She took a few cautious steps and noticed all there was in that little room was a ladder to her left.

Everything was blank, and everything was black.

"Huh."

Zaraquel glanced at the ladder once more and hesitated before continuing. The whispers got louder, almost as if the woman spoke in her ear. Startled, she jumped.

"Do it," the voice said. "Do it."

She didn't think twice as she lowered herself down and grabbed onto the sides of the ladder, and descended. "Shit, it's dark."

"Keep going," the voice urged. It sounded almost desperate, pleading.

Not wanting to let fear get in the way, Zaraquel continued. "I have to. For Rae."

Moments later, she took one final step before her feet hit the floor. She surveyed the space. She was now underground somehow as if that ladder had transported her into an alternate universe.

"Whoa." She stood face to face with a massive hole, or...well, what used to be a hole.

She touched it—it was hot. "Ow, what the hell?" Zaraquel stepped back, the tip of her finger in her mouth, as she tried to alleviate some of the pain that came with the burn.

That giant hole had been filled, but why? Her mind

turned with different possibilities and landed on one. Eyes wide and mouth agape, she said, "Fuck."

She distanced herself from the hole and paced back and forth around the room. "No. No. No. No. That's impossible. It can't be it. No, not the portal again." Zaraquel quickly glanced at it. "It makes sense, though," she tried to talk some sense into herself.

"Turn around," the voice rushed out.

She whipped her head around to face the portal. She waited for something groundbreaking to happen, and all that met her was silence. Nothing but silence.

That's when she saw it. Beside the portal was a glowing symbol. Zaraquel walked closer to inspect it.

"I can't believe it, just like in the books. It's a unicursal hexagram!"

On impulse, Zaraquel placed her finger on the sigil and pushed it deeper into the wall. There was a bright, blinding glow that emanated from the symbols. She cowered as she covered her eyes.

***

Nimue

There was a sort of tingling sensation as if Nimue felt every part of her body waking up. The hair on her arms stood to attention, and she was suddenly aware of her surroundings. First, it was cool and dark—an emptiness. A rush of wind came at her in full force, and Nimue tried to clutch onto something substantial, but there was nothing to be found as she was being plucked from obscurity. She moved at such an amazingly fast velocity that she felt her skin stretch backward, reaching its capacity.

Then, it was bright and warm. It was incredibly hot, so much so that she had to close her eyes. When she opened them, she found a pair of round, confused eyes that stared right back at her. A young woman. *But how?*

"W…Who are you?" The young woman with the long hair spoke to her.

Nimue warily examined her surroundings. It wasn't hot anymore, but the opposite as before, in the darkness. She tried to move her feet and felt the gravel and dirt in between her toes.

The girl spoke up louder this time. "Who are you?"

Suddenly Nimue felt the ground shake beneath her feet violently, and the dark room which held her captive spun around and around. She cradled her head in her hands and tried to gain some semblance of control. It was all too much.

Too much.

"I…I…." Nimue wanted so desperately to speak, but nothing came out of her mouth.

She lost her balance and fell to the ground. Her world was black once more.

***

Zaraquel

A woman appearing from nowhere in the blink of an eye was the last thing Zaraquel expected when she pressed the sigil. And the same young woman was now on the ground. Zaraquel noticed that they looked to be the same age.

"Shit." Quickly, she crouched down to see if this mystery woman was breathing. She placed her fingers on her neck. Her pulse was slow but steady. "Ah, thank God she's alive."

Zaraquel jumped to her feet and immediately paced across the room. Crap. She was going to get in so much trouble. "Some rando just popped into The Order, yeah, no big deal," she scoffed at herself. "Dad, Mom.... Oh, my God. And then there's Uncle Mac." She paused. "Wait, wait a minute. Uncle Mac."

Could he have sent the woman without Zaraquel not knowing? And her just pressing the button and the woman appearing was a coincidence?

"Yeah, that's it. Has to be." She needed to convince herself that this was the reason. Now the question was, how the hell was she going to get this woman some help? She searched the recesses of her mind as if she had a Rolodex full of spells at her disposal. She closed her eyes, and Zaraquel felt her eyeballs moving from side to side rapidly.

"*Securus onerariam*" left her lips like a prayer.

Zaraquel turned in time to see the woman slowly fade and disappear into her chosen location—the guest room intended for new recruits. Her search for the perfect spell to bring back Rae had failed. As a warrior, it was her duty to protect and save the innocent. That woman, whomever she was, was innocent. At least she thought she was.

So, as Zaraquel made her way back to where she had come from, she made sure that everything was as Uncle Mac left it. Satisfied, she headed to the guest wing.

She quietly opened the door and found the woman in a deep sleep. She took a few steps inside and sat beside her. It was troubling, though. The woman tossed and turned, and her skin was blanketed with sweat.

Zaraquel, concerned with the woman's well-being, took hold of her hand. She thought holding her hand would quash the woman's tossing and turning.

***

Nimue

As she felt a slight pressure on her hand, Nimue wanted her eyes to open, but they wouldn't. There was some sort of disconnect between her brain and her body. It was as if someone or something sat on top of her, weighed her down, kept her from moving.

She wanted to, but she physically couldn't.

Suddenly, she was bombarded with images that didn't really make sense to her, like a nightmare with missing puzzle pieces. In this dream, she saw a Tall Dark Man emerging from the shadows. He talked to her with a certain familiarity.

"Nimue."

Who's Nimue? She looked around the dark void, but there was no one to be found.

He continued, his presence cowering over her. "The portal is for your use only. You must continue with the plan."

The plan? What plan?

However, when she opened her mouth to respond to this man, she was unable to speak. Her voice was lost, as was her recollection of the man before her. Just as quickly as he had appeared, he disappeared with only a few parting words that she made out, "Zaraquel," "dark forces," "angel is mine."

She ran around in the darkness and looked for the entity that had approached, yet only found that her voice had returned, "Hello? Hello, are you out there?"

It seemed he'd left her with more questions than answers.

THUNK! Her dream world shook as if there was an earthquake. Nimue looked up to what she considered to be the sky in the abundant darkness and saw that there was a large crack.

***

Zaraquel

"Oh no." Zaraquel jumped to her feet when she saw the woman convulsing on the bed. With harsh movements, her limbs jerked, and she flailed uncontrollably, and grasped onto the sheets beneath her.

The stranger began to float and rose from the bed like a broken doll, her arms dangling below her. Without a second thought, Zaraquel unfurled her wings and flew up to save her from falling to the floor. She gently cradled her in her arms, "Don't worry, I got you."

As Zaraquel floated down with the woman in her grasp, her eyes burst open, and what Zaraquel saw was something she'd never witnessed before: the woman's eyes were glowing white. Her body sagged against Zaraquel's hold as if she had given up, and she closed her eyes.

Zaraquel set her down on the bed. Her hands shook

with nervous energy. Never in her research or in her personal experience had she witnessed such an event. But here she was, beside a mysterious woman whose eyes glowed.

CHAPTER 3

Zaraquel

"What the hell just happened?" Zaraquel murmured to herself as she flitted through the kitchen. She didn't know how to cook, but she knew how to press Start on the microwave, and that's what she did. As she rifled through the kitchen cabinets to find a can of soup, her thoughts ran a thousand miles a minute. She had never seen such a phenomenon, never knew such a thing could happen. The woman had looked possessed as she floated above the bed.

Zaraquel found what she was looking for, popped open the can, and poured it into a bowl. After two minutes in the microwave, she gently climbed the stairs and brought her guest some food.

"This should do her some good," she said, proud of her culinary feat.

She gently kicked the door open with her foot and saw

her mother next to the sleeping stranger. She lost her grip on the bowl, and it fell, but her mother, with a flick of her hand, made the bowl float. It suspended in the air and landed on the nightstand, the steam ring from the heat.

"Zaraquel." Her lips were a straight line and her brows furrowed; her mother spoke her name in the way only a mother could. "Follow me outside, *now*."

"B...but her soup."

"You can heat it up later *after* you explain yourself, young lady."

Begrudgingly Zaraquel followed her, scared of her fate. Nothing scared her more than when her mother was angry. She even thought her mother could be scarier than the Tall Dark Man. She tried to suppress a giggle, but when she imagined the Tall Dark Man cowering in a corner, facing her mother, the giggle slipped. This caused another hard stare from her mother.

***

Chloe

As they reached Zaraquel's room, Chloe paced back and forth, from one end of the room to the other. The moment she had entered her house to check on Zaraquel, she knew something was wrong — she *felt* it.

The overall energy of the house felt cold and murky as if something evil or dark clouded the goodness that emanated from the walls. So she did what any concerned mother would do — she checked for signs of danger. Unlike most mothers, she was also a witch. Chloe cast a spell that sought the darkness, and immediately a puff of dark smoke made a trail up the stairs and into the room where the woman slept.

She looked down at her and noticed the woman stirred in her sleep as if something weighed heavily on her. The more Chloe studied her, however, the more she realized this woman seemed incredibly familiar to her. She could not place her face.

Determined to figure out who she was, she enacted a spell her mother had taught her, and with one touch, she knew a person's intentions — the truth could not be hidden. Chloe gingerly placed one hand on the woman's shoulder and was assaulted with a mental block. It was so strong the only thing she was allowed to feel was fear. Fear of what, she had no idea. Chloe was flung across the room by an immense force before she could find out.

Whoever this woman is, she thought to herself, *she possesses great power.* Chloe was not the kind of witch to give up easily. She took a deep breath and called upon her ancestor, Sarah Good, a powerful witch in her bloodline, to give her the strength to see this woman's intentions. Again, she was hit by the same powerful force that prevented her from finding out the truth.

Her fists curled at her sides at the memory of what had happened moments before. She turned to her daughter, who sat on her bed, face down, looking at her shoes as if they were the most interesting thing in the world.

"Zaraquel, how could you possibly think that bringing a stranger into The Order would be okay?

"I know. I know. But in my defense, I totally thought

that Uncle Mac zapped her in."

"Right," Chloe said, unconvinced. "So you thought he sent someone so powerful, without him here to guide her? Alone?"

"H...how do you know she's powerful?" She leapt up to her feet. "Did she do something else?"

Chloe arched a brow, "Define 'something else.'"

"Shit."

"*Zaraquel.*"

"Sorry, Mom. Look, okay. She looked tired, so obviously, she needed to rest, right? So, I let her into the room to sleep. Thirty minutes in, I went to check on her, and she convulsed, grabbed onto the sheets and everything. Then suddenly, she floated in the air, and her eyes glowed. They glowed white. I couldn't believe it! And well, then she stopped and went back to sleep."

"Zaraquel, Mac may have sent her. I don't know. I don't have a good feeling about her."

"C'mon, Mom. Aren't you and Dad always saying we should help others with our gifts? That's what I'm trying to do here. To help her."

"And, that's very admirable, sweetheart, but we need to be careful here. We don't know who she is, where she's from, or what she is capable of. We are still recovering from the battle. We won, but we also lost our friends."

"So, what? We're just gonna kick her to the curb and say, 'See ya, have a nice life'?"

"Zaraquel, don't start. Be reasonable."

"Mom! She needs our help!"

"Do *not* raise your voice at me, Z."

They stared at each other, fire in their eyes, neither one willing to let it go. This was their pattern when they had disagreements.

Chloe shook her head and relented. "You can only see her if you're supervised."

Zaraquel rolled her eyes and protested. "You're overreacting, Mom."

"I found my daughter in our house alone with a complete stranger, and you accuse me of overreacting? Don't push it, Zaraquel." Chloe looked around Zaraquel's room—clothes all strewn on the floor, ingredients of potions on her desk. She sighed. "And please, clean your room. I have to track Mac down and see what's going on."

She stepped out and closed the door. Chloe didn't expect Zaraquel to be so adamant about this woman. But she was—she was so eager to help someone, to save someone, that Chloe became even more worried.

What if she lost her daughter to grief? In her heart, she wished that Rae hadn't died so that her daughter would still be happy and whole, like before.

**

Nimue

Days after she received help from the girl and her parents, Nimue felt strong enough to get up from the bed. The kindness from these strangers that fed her and cared for her was something she'd never experienced before. A sort of warmth enveloped her being. She didn't know what to make of it.

Nor did she know what force had attacked her body. She only remembered what happened in bits and pieces, never a concrete thought. Her body felt rigid, and she couldn't control her actions. She was a puppet being pulled in different directions. She tried to stitch her memories together, but something or someone prevented her from doing so. Was her brain too fragmented after the attack? She didn't know, but she was scared to find out. What if what she discovered was far worse than she imagined?

What Nimue needed to do was distract herself, and she thought a nice walk outside would do the trick. When she felt the blades of grass touch her feet, a sudden glee filled her, and laughter bubbled in her chest.

The sunrays hit her skin, and she felt glorious. She felt alive. So, with arms spread out, she spun in a circle, round and round and round, until she dizzily fell to the ground. She felt light, carefree—a blank slate. Nimue opened her eyes only to find that someone was blocking her view: a woman. *The* woman, her angel.

She smiled down at her. "You're finally up!"

Nimue looked down shyly. "Um, yes. I couldn't stay in bed any longer. My muscles felt stiff."

"I get that." She plopped down next to her and bumped her shoulder with hers. "I'm Zaraquel, by the way."

"Nimue."

"Cool name."

"I could say the same."

They shared a smile and enjoyed the scenic view of

the grounds. In the comfortable silence, Nimue surveyed her surroundings and saw different magical beings in the middle of practice. There were wolves, in and out of human form. Vampires appeared from one end of the area to the next, and it looked like they practiced for something. She noticed that this area was specially built to protect the vampires. And lastly, the witches. Nimue saw clearly that this was a safe haven for the magical community. She even saw that they were all friendly with one another, laughing and bonding. Nimue wondered where she'd ended up.

She felt Zaraquel staring at her, so she turned. "What?"

With a curious stare, she replied. "I'm trying to figure out what you are."

What you are. What you are. What you are.

At the sound of that phrase, Nimue drifted into the past.

***

Nimue, 1276

She was bombarded with memories — they replayed in her head as if she had watched a movie about her life. She was an observer who watched a younger version of herself. She walked in and around the memory, but no one saw her or heard her. It was an astounding thing.

The vision seemed familiar and foreign all the same. Nimue saw herself in the middle of a forest, much like the one she was situated in currently. But in her memory, everything looked newer, greener. There was magic in the air, and she felt it.

Someone tapped on her shoulder, and she whipped around to see who it is. It was a tall man with dark hair and a warm smile. She saw herself play with the string of his robe, and the man smirked at the interaction. He took a step back, and she followed.

"Why, Nimue, if I didn't know you any better, I would think you want something."

"We all want something. It's the natural order of things, M—"

Nimue couldn't hear the name that was spoken—it was as if her ability to hear had disappeared. She felt sick to the pit of her stomach and knew something was off. She couldn't quite pinpoint it, but it was the same dread she had felt when her body seized.

The conversation shifted in and out of silence. So she approached them, hoping this would help, but it didn't. In fact, it was worse. And to make matters more frustrating, Nimue couldn't read lips.

And then with a *SWOOSH!* sound commenced. As the Nimue from the memory walked around the man, as a predator did to her prey, she traced the width of his back with the tip of her finger. She stopped and whispered in his ear, "You know you want to show me. Do it."

He shook his head with a trembling breath. "No."

"You know you can; I've seen you."

"You're right. I can. But I choose not to. I don't know if you can be trusted. I don't know what you are."

***

Nimue, Present Day

I don't know what you are. What you are. What you are. The words echoed in her ears as she snapped out of her reverie.

"Helllllooo, Nimue?"

She blinked a few times. "Zaraquel?"

"Yes?"

"You're here." She looked around. The witches, the werewolves, the vampires were all there. Zaraquel was still there. Nimue was confused and a little pale. She even began to feel a little nauseous.

"Nimue, are you okay? You went somewhere, where did you go?

Still discombobulated, she dug her hands into the dirt, literally grounding herself to something real, something tangible.

"Here. Here, but not here. Does that make sense?

Zaraquel chuckled nervously. "Uh no, not really."

Suddenly a stray fireball, courtesy of the witches' training, flew in their direction.

With a wave of her hand, Nimue made a forcefield and shielded them—by the looks of it, half the field as well. Everyone, including Zaraquel, looked at Nimue with great interest. By their expressions of bewilderment, she sensed their awe. Uncomfortable, she shifted in her seat, dropped her hand, and the forcefield fell.

She stood and walked off the field and into the house. Zaraquel followed not too far behind.

***

Zaraquel

She buzzed with excitement as she entered the house.

"*Whoa*. Whoa. That was so cool! I mean, seriously, SO. COOL. Can you teach me that? How did you do that, anyway? You didn't even say an incantation. I was there. I would've heard you."

Nimue held onto the banister, as that move made her weak. Her knees trembled, and she quickly sat down on the steps.

"Are you okay, Nimue?"

"I'm fine. I'm sure it'll pass."

"Are you sure?"

Nimue nodded, so Zaraquel leapt to her feet and began her inquisition once more.

"I...I still don't know how you did it. Half the field and it didn't even look like you were trying. You just did it. That's amazing!" She took a breath, hoping to tamper her excitement, but it didn't work. "So, can you teach me?"

"Can she teach you what?" Her mom stepped out from the kitchen, flour on her apron.

"Are you making cookies?"

Chloe smirked, "Maybe." She dusted her hands off. "Where's your dad? I thought he was with you."

"He was, we just came inside for a bit, right, Nimue?"

Nimue nodded in response.

"Now, what did you want her to teach you?"

Zaraquel jumped at the chance to recount her tale. Meanwhile, Chloe looked back and forth between Zaraquel and Nimue.

"Really? Half of the field, is that so?"

"Totally. Mom, it was crazy!"

"Huh."

Zaraquel knew that tone, the speculating kind her mother used when she was not entirely convinced.

"Mom, don't."

Chloe took a seat beside Nimue, and Zaraquel noticed her hands tightly clasped on her

lap. "What spell did you use, hmmm?"

Nimue avoided her mother's stare and whispered, "I didn't."

"What?" Chloe queried. "That's impossible." She took a second as if constructing an idea in her mind. "What did you say your name was?"

And again, Nimue responded. "I didn't."

Not a big fan of the mind games adults played, Zaraquel cut to the chase. "It's Nimue."

Her mother froze at the mention of her name and abruptly stood. She tucked a loose strand behind her ear, and Zaraquel knew she only did that when she was nervous or scared.

"Mom?"

"Uh, I gotta check the cookies." She watched her mom scurry back into the kitchen.

***

Zaraquel

Days later, her mother was still skittish around her new powerful friend. They didn't think she knew, but she knew very well that her parents kept a vigilant eye on Nimue.

She was powerful, so what?

What if she taught the witches something new? From a different perspective? That's when the idea occurred to her. Nimue was powerful, and therefore, she could help her with the little Rae problem. Perhaps she was even powerful enough to bring her back. Zaraquel didn't know, but she had to try.

With a silent motion, Zaraquel gestured for Nimue to follow her, which she did without question. They made their way deep into the forest, far from the practice fields, and stopped at a clearing.

"I want you to teach me."

Nimue quizzically looked at her. "Teach you what?"

"Teach me everything you know."

"I...I don't even know what I know."

"Then how did you protect us from the fireball? I don't understand."

"Neither do I," Nimue replied honestly. "It's like my body knew what it was doing before even thinking about it."

"Like an instinct."

"Exactly. Like...like muscle memory. I just thought I could stop the fireball, and I did. It just happened."

"Huh. Can you try it now?"

Zaraquel was curious about Nimue's technique, so she observed her closely. While Nimue stood still and closed her eyes, presumably to focus, Zaraquel noticed her stance. Her posture was relaxed as if magic were as easy as breathing.

Noticing the rise and fall of her chest, she immediately realized when Nimue stopped breathing.

***

Nimue

She felt the air escape her lungs and get caught in her throat. She was stuck and unable to move when she heard *his* voice. The man from her dream, the Tall Dark Man. His voice was faint, but she heard it. It was clear to her.

"Now's your chance," he whispered.

My chance to what? She thought to herself and waited for him to answer.

He did. "Remember…your magic."

And just as quickly as her breath was taken away, oxygen returned to her body. She took breaths, and with every breath, her memory of magic, her skills became clearer. All the lessons learned and the spells invented were back in her head where they belonged. She didn't know how she learned them or who taught her—they just appeared as if they'd always been there.

She felt at peace in remembering her magic, her power. This sense of independence made her feel empowered and free. But something still didn't feel right. Her skin crawled with goosebumps.

At that moment, she tried to remember her actual life, outside of the magic. Who was she? Who did she belong to? Why did she feel this deep emptiness?

She pushed her mind to open, but she was hitting a block. She now knew that it was a magical barrier—someone was keeping her from remembering who she was. Yes, she remembered the magic, but that was not all that made her, her—was it?

There had to be more. She was more than the power that magic made her feel. She saw that in the grounds of the Order. There was an entire community of magical beings that not only embraced their power but lifted each other up. She wanted that more than she was willing to admit.

With a snap of Zaraquel's finger, Nimue opened her eyes. It was as if a fire were lit inside of, and she had a new lease on life, and she was excited to live and to share her magic.

"All right, let's do this."

"I...I thought you said you didn't remember."

She didn't want to scare Zarquel, so she knowingly shied away from the truth. "Ummm. I willed myself to remember, and I did."

"Seriously? Shut the front door! Now you *really* gotta teach me!"

Nimue chuckled at Zaraquel's eagerness. "Now, let's go over what you know, and then we'll take it from there."

They covered the basics: casting spells, making and gathering ingredients for potions, flying, etc. Nimue was surprised at Zaraquel's level of skill—she was truly quite the little warrior.

"It seems like you're off to a good start."

Her eyes bugged out in confusion, "'Good start'?"

"Well, that's why you came out here with me, wasn't it? To learn? To be more powerful?"

"Can you read minds too?"

At this, Nimue let out a heartfelt laugh. "No, but can I tell you a secret?" Zaraquel nodded, and Nimue leaned and whispered, "I wish I could."

They shared a laugh and made a plan to meet after hours from now on.

CHAPTER 4

Zaraquel

There was a whole other side to magic that Zaraquel never knew about. As she walked out to meet Nimue at their spot, the nerves hit her, as they had for the past few days. She knew she shouldn't be doing this. And yes, she had the books, but she had reached a point where she was unable to decipher them. She needed help, specifically Nimue's, to get Rae back.

If there was one person that knew how to do that, it was her extremely powerful mentor. With the books under her arm, tonight was the night: she was going to tell her why she wanted to learn more, to *be* more.

She *needed* Rae back.

Her mind raced with possibilities of how Nimue would react, the truth behind her motives. When she arrived and noticed Nimue in deep concentration, she stopped in her tracks. It was not the fact that Nimue floated mid-air, but everything else was still. Nothing was moving. There was complete silence.

Everything was frozen.

The birds were still in the air, the water from the creek nearby was quiet, not one sound. The elements listened to her, and even a novice would know it took a special kind of person to harness that amount of power.

Zaraquel was amazed. "Wow."

She knew that this power, the dark magic as Uncle Mac and her mom called it, was disbanded and forbidden to be practiced. She knew this, yet she continued to soldier on as Nimue made her way back down, her feet touching the ground. Zaraquel's eyes glittered with excitement as Nimue approached her.

"You're late."

"Yeah, sorry, I was getting a few things."

"You're ready then to begin?" Nimue prodded. She nodded so fast and hard she felt a bit dizzy. Nimue held on to her shoulders, balancing her. "Easy now, Zaraquel."

"Right. Right. I can do that." She took a few calming breaths, and her world felt right once more.

Nimue gestured to the books in her hand. "I see you have some new materials."

"Yeah, they're just something I found, y'know, lying around." She shrugged nonchalantly.

"Right." Nimue raised a skeptical brow but reached for the books anyway. "Let me see." She flipped through the pages, intrigued at the old magic and rituals described. "And where exactly did you 'find' these?"

Zaraquel kicked a pebble with her shoe. "Around."

Nimue grabbed Zaraquel by the chin. "This is serious magic. The oldest kind, Zaraquel. I assumed you wanted to learn defense *against* the dark arts."

Her patience was running thin. "I just saw you floating, y'know, in sole command of the elements. I'm not *that* naive—I know you used dark magic, okay. You just have to teach me."

"I don't *have* to do anything." Nimue stalled from teaching her, and this pissed her off.

Zaraquel took this chance to grab her wrist. "Please, please don't go." Her voice broke with tears, "I...I need you."

Nimue turned to face her. "Why? Why do you need me?"

Her eyes filled with tears. "I need to get her back, my best friend. It...It's like, I don't know, a part of me is missing, and I can't even breathe."

She crashed down and fell into herself, her arms clenched around her stomach. Zaraquel was tired of pretending everything was okay.

***

Nimue

Nimue wanted to walk away, to save Zaraquel from the turmoil of the dark magic. But she heard him again, the Tall Dark Man, telling her to stay. She tried to push back and move, but she couldn't.

He wanted her to stay, so she did. She couldn't recall why he sounded urgent about this.

The moment she heard the anguish in Zaraquel's

voice, however, it broke her heart. Nimue knew very well how Zaraquel felt. She sat beside her and gently pulled her in, Zaraquel's head resting on her shoulder.

"I understand, believe me, I do."

She sniffled. "You do? You lost someone?"

I lost myself.

"Yes, but I'm trying to get her back."

Zaraquel perked up. "So, you see what I'm trying to do. You understand."

"Yes. In these pages," Nimue propped open the books, "Lies the lost language of magic, the very first of its kind."

"And you can read it?"

"I can, but I don't know why."

"Like your magic, you just know?" Zaraquel pondered.

"Yes." She flipped through the book and found what she was looking for. "This. This right here, for example, is a resurrection spell."

Zaraquel grabbed the book. "You did it! You found it!" The words looked like gibberish to her, nonetheless. "I still can't read it. Why?"

Nimue sighed, knowing the truth would reveal her true nature, the one she was trying to fight, but she told her anyway. She deserved to know what she's walking into. "Only the ones who have been on the Path of Darkness can read this particular section."

"Oh, so you've always used dark magic then?"

She looked away, ashamed. "In a way, yes." She didn't want to face her truth, so she changed the subject. "Tell me about your friend."

"Rae?"

"Yes, I want to hear all about her. She must be pretty special to be considered as your best friend."

"She was." They shared a small smile and talk about the girls' friendship.

***

Zaraquel

Zaraquel let out a defeated sigh as Nimue focused on defense training rather than addressing the book as she had before. She knew what Nimue was doing, though Zaraquel was far too smart to be thrown off. With every attack that Nimue threw her way, Zaraquel grew more and more frustrated.

She wanted Rae back, and she wanted her *now!*

But this time, instead of blocking Nimue, she fought, attacked her with a gust of wind. The forces collided and rippled through the property, causing both women to fall on opposite ends.

Nimue stood and brushed herself off. "Zaraquel, what do you think you're doing?"

"I'm tired of you dodging the subject. You know what I want, so why don't you teach me?!" Zaraquel flew up to Nimue, so close to her that she corralled her in with her wings.

"Zaraquel, calm down," Nimue pleaded.

"No, I will not! I just want her to come back, goddammit!"

"Yes, but are you willing to go through with the consequences?"

Zaraquel closed her wings, disappointed. "What are you talking about?"

"The spell is not for the faint of heart."

"I am stronger than you think, Nimue."

"You are strong. I know that, Zaraquel. Never for one moment since we met have I thought otherwise. But this is different."

She raised her chin in defiance. "So?"

"So, are you willing to sacrifice another soul?"

Zaraquel was hit with the memory of Auntie Amber being resurrected—after all, that was her purpose. Had she been so blind she didn't remember the stipulations? "A life for a life."

"Exactly." Nimue nodded. "But this spell is different because it is one of the first. It's messier, more damaging to the soul."

"What are you talking about?"

Nimue's gaze hadn't wavered, and Zaraquel wanted to flinch, but she didn't. Nimue continued. "Because your friend was an innocent, the sacrifice needs to be an innocent."

She felt the weight of the world bringing her down, more than it had before. Her hopes, once alive and bright, were now shattered. She was lost and confused. She looked up to the heavens and thought, *What should I do?*

Zaraquel's breaths became more shallow.

"Are you willing to do that, Z?" Nimue asked.

At the sound of her old nickname from her new friend, she remembered Rae, giggling as Zaraquel tackled her with tickles one early morning. Zaraquel closed the distance and placed her forearm against Nimue's throat. "Don't call me that."

Nimue raised her hands in surrender. "Zaraquel, I'm trying t—"

"Get away from her!" Zaraquel heard her mom yell, fury in her voice.

Both turned only to see Zaraquel's parents with Malakai, Amber, and Uncle Mac. All were in pajamas, save for Uncle Mac, who she assumed had just arrived.

With her arm still firmly placed on Nimue's throat, she asked, "W...what are you guys doing here?"

"Don't even get me started, Zaraquel," her mother seethed.

"Mom, I—" Zaraquel sputtered, disappointed she'd gotten caught.

Her father continued where her mother left off. "We specifically told you *not* to be around *her* unsupervised.

"But—"

She looked around, and they had created a perimeter around them, caging them in. *What are they doing?*

"Look, I just wanted some extra lessons, and Nimue here offered to help." She turned to Nimue and lowered her arm, freeing her. "Right, Nimue?"

"Yes." Nimue looked away, only to have Uncle Mac step up to them. He held Nimue's face with a tight grip, so tight that Zaraquel was afraid for her new friend. Mal motioned for Zaraquel to stand beside him.. Zaraquel noticed that they were all against Nimue, and yet she felt like they were taking it out on her. Amber's birthmark was glowing, her mother clenched her fists, her father was snarling, and Mal was being overprotective. Tensions were high, and she was nervous, so she did as he said, but she was more confused than she was before. Her soul was hurting more now than just for the death of Rae.

***

Nimue

The man's hands felt rough, cold against her skin. She squirmed, but he whispered, *"In clausa."* She couldn't move. Her hands fused to the tree.

He turned and addressed the group. "You were right, Chloe. It's her." And back to Nimue, he said, "How? How is this possible?"

She quirked a brow in confusion. "Who are you?"

The man laughed incredulously. "C'mon, Nimue, don't play dumb. We both know you're much smarter than that."

He talked to her as if he knew her. *What could he possibly know?* she wondered.

She had to find out, but she needed to release herself if she wanted to do just that. She closed her eyes and took in a deep breath. As she exhaled, she felt her molecules separate and felt lighter than air. At that point, she knew she had broken the spell and unattached herself from the tree.

"Do you know who I am?" she queried.

The man rolled his eyes, "You're not fooling anyone. *Est alligatum.*"

Suddenly chains appeared, tightening every time she

moved. It hurt her as if her skin were being pulled apart from her bones. She groaned in terrible agony.

"Stop! You're hurting her!" Zaraquel yelled in her defense. She saw a redheaded woman holding her back.

The man walked over to Zaraquel. "C'mon, Uncle Mac, why are you doing this?"

He pointed to her, and Nimue felt small. All the people looked at her with such disdain, such rage. She felt misunderstood. Again.

The man, now revealed to be Uncle Mac, continued. "That woman you see there is none other than the Nimue of legend."

"I...I don't get it."

"She was a true witch, the purest of our kind, and she was great—magnificent even. She had it all: intelligence, power, beauty."

Nimue squirmed; she didn't like unwanted attention. Yet here they were, talking about her as if they knew her. *She* didn't even know who she was. How could they?

Uncle Mac proceeded, his glare even more intense than before. "But it wasn't enough, was it?" He walked up to her and, with a wave of his hand, lifted her body to stand. She groaned as the chains tightened. "You wanted more."

"More of what?" She gasped.

"More power, more *life*," he spat. "You sold your soul."

She wanted to know, even if it hurt. "To who?"

"The Tall Dark Man. Nimue is nothing but vile and wicked." She heard Zaraquel gasp in shock. She looked at Zaraquel only to find her flying away. Her family yelled for her to return, but she didn't. She flew away and left her. She left her with these people who saw her as a threat.

Could what he had said be true. Was she evil?

All she felt before she closed her eyes was unbearable pain. Like the howling of the wind, her screams filled the night sky.

CHAPTER 5

Zaraquel

Could what Uncle Mac said be true? Zaraquel thought to herself as she flew further away from them. They had only known each other for such a brief time, but there was something profound that connected them.

Nimue's screams were all Zaraquel heard as she ventured off into the clouds. Zaraquel stopped, floating in mid-air, and took a brief reprieve from all that was around her. Her parents, forgotten; the supposed threat that loomed around Nimue; even the memory of Rae, if for a moment, was placed on the back burner.

Zaraquel collected herself in the peace and tranquility the open space had to offer her. She focused on the gentle, constant flapping of her wings on her breath as it moved in and out of her chest. She couldn't quite pinpoint why, but she knew with certainty she had to fly back, so she did.

The wind ruffled her feathers at the furious speed at which she moved, but Zaraquel no longer cared. Nimue needed her.

It's nice to be needed, again. A bittersweet smile lit her face. The thought quickly vanished when she reached the ground, inches away from Nimue.

"Stay away from her!" she ordered as the adults tightened the perimeter around her. Uncle Mac maintained his magical hold on Nimue while her parents tried to convince her to get out of the way.

"Zaraquel, you need to move *now*," her mother seethed.

Her dad attempted to placate her. "It's for the best, honey."

It didn't work. Zaraquel couldn't take it anymore—the loss of Rae and the potential loss of Nimue took its toll on her.

Suddenly, behind her, she heard Nimue's voice as she weakly said, "Stop. Zaraquel." Her voice was broken, "If what they say is true, let them do what they must."

At hearing the defeat from her cries, Zaraquel whipped around to face Nimue. She shook her head no in hopes that Nimue understood how much she meant to her now. She faced her family with tears in her eyes, "I'm not gonna let you take another friend from me!"

Her mother's expression softened as she quickly shared a look with her father. Meanwhile, Amber and Malakai looked morosely at the ground. Uncle Mac, however, broke the silence, looking at Nimue.

"She is *no* friend." He then waved a hand over Zaraquel, *"Altum somnum."*

Zaraquel's breathing slowed down as she began to fall. Her father swooped in to catch her before she hit the ground. Her body felt weightless as she was lulled into a deep sleep and her eyes finally closed, the dark sky engulfing her.

***

Nimue

Knowing her family would never harm Zaraquel, Nimue knew she would be fine. Nevertheless, she still worried for her new friend. She never had a friend before, a friend like Zaraquel. As she looked around in the cold, damp room, which they hauled her into not long after Zaraquel was taken away, she feared she would never again see her little witch.

Had Zaraquel not found her the day she did, Nimue shuttered to think about what her fate might have been. Forever alone, without a clue. Now that she thought about it, however, not much had changed, given she was held as a prisoner far from the premises of The Order.

The dense air and cold climate made her believe she was once more somewhere underground. She was bound by a circle of salt and a few other protection charms as she sat on the ground, her bare feet beneath her. She rocked herself back and forth to soothe her wandering mind.

She heard footsteps in the distance and knew her captors had returned. Nimue turned as they neared and faced the man who held her with so much disdain — Mac, she believed was his name — as well as the red-headed woman beside him. There was something different about her, though. Her aura was peculiar. Nimue sensed it as if the woman herself had lived a thousand lives before.

Interesting.

They circled her like vultures stalking their prey. She could very easily escape, but her morbid curiosity got the best of her, and she wanted to discover what it was they thought they knew.

"What are you doing here, Nimue?" Mac asked.

"I...I don't know."

"Don't bullshit me, Nimue," he growled.

The woman shook her head in disapproval. "Mac."

"No, Amber! She doesn't get to sit here and play victim after all she has done."

Huh, so her name is Amber. It suits her.

Mac ran a hand through his hair, fists clenched at his sides. Meanwhile, Amber crouched down to meet her gaze. She was analyzing her, trying to penetrate her mind. Nimue could feel it—her futile effort was laughable.

But much like herself, Amber was unable to make sense of her muddled thoughts.

"I can't read her thoughts. I mean, I can, but it's like her brain, her memories, are fragmented."

"Of course," Mac muttered. "She did that on purpose, a defense mechanism. Don't you see that?"

"I don't think so."

This was her chance to speak up, so she did. "I don't know how I got here. All I know is that Zaraquel was the first person I saw."

"Like she woke you up?" Amber asked.

"Yes," Nimue confirmed with a firm nod.

***

Zaraquel

With arms stretched overhead, Zaraquel yawned as the sunshine streamed through and stretched wide. It was warm. The gentle light signified the start of a new day. But the memory of leaving Nimue behind with her family hit Zaraquel deep in the gut. She knew she would never leave Rae behind, yet she'd left her new friend. The guilt was a powerful tool that weakened her spirit.

She turned and buried her head in the pillow, tears streaming down her cheeks. "Oh, Nimue."

She heard the sound of her bedroom door creak open, and she lay still. By their hushed whispers, she knew it was her parents coming in to check on her. After what they did, however, Zaraquel did not want to talk to them, much less see them.

"Zaraquel." Her mother sat down on the bed beside her. "I know you're awake, sweetie."

"Zaraquel isn't here at the moment. Can I take a message?" She turned only enough to open one eye. She saw her father smirk while her mother rolled her eyes and stared at the ceiling a moment too long.

"Very funny, Z." Her father took a seat beside them. "C'mon, we gotta talk."

Turning on her back, she groaned, truly dreading this conversation. Her eyes darted across the room, looking at everything except her parents' eyes.

"Do we have to?" she whined. "I haven't even had a

proper breakfast yet."

"You will," he said, "*after*."

She sighed. "Alriiiiiight." She sat up with a huff. "Hit me."

Her parents shared a look and settled in their seats, their once sympathetic expressions now serious.

"You deliberately disobeyed us, Zaraquel."

"I know, Mom." She sank back into her seat, settled deep into the pillows.

"Yes, you *know* this, and you still did it? I don't understand." The static in the air was thick, and her mom's hair began to float, her anger rising to the surface.

"You never understood," Zaraquel muttered through thin lips.

With a warning tone, Chloe said, "Zaraquel...."

Her father placed a hand on her mother's shoulder, and she visibly relaxed, her hair returning to its normal state. He soldiered on with what needed to be said. "First, we were and still are concerned about your safety. That's our number one priority, your safety."

"I know, b--"

He raised his hand, "I'm not finished. Being with Nimue here, she jeopardized you and our family. We do not know what she is fully capable of."

"You have no idea." The admission slipped out from Zaraquel. She clamped her mouth shut and stopped talking immediately.

"Exactly. That's even more of a reason to stay away from her," her mother interjected.

"But—" Zaraquel stopped herself before she revealed anything else.

"But, what?" her mother asked, suspicious of her motives.

But I need her. Rae needs her.

***

Nimue

Still in the circle—but now, thanks to Amber, she sat in a chair—Nimue remained their willing prisoner. She could very easily unbind the spell and get out of there, but she didn't want to leave Zaraquel.

What also piqued her interest was Mac. She felt his magic—he was well trained. His maneuvers and enunciation of the spell casting seemed familiar to her, but like everything else in her life, she couldn't place it.

Watching as Mac paced the room, she caught bits, and pieces of the whispered conversation shared between Mac and Amber.

"She doesn't remember, Mac. We can't keep her here."

"That's what she wants us to think, Amber. She's a master of deception—this is what she does."

"And if she's telling the truth?"

She was. She wanted to scream across the room loud enough to shake the walls. She didn't, but she wanted to. Nimue didn't know who or what she was, but she was certain those two would find out. They were too powerful not to.

"A truth spell." The idea left her lips quickly.

Mac stopped and perked up at the sound of her voice.

"What was that?" They walked toward her, and for some reason, she found herself sitting up straighter in her seat.

"Truth spell. Do it."

"That's actually a good idea," Amber mused.

"I happen to have them on occasion."

Amber laughed in response, but it died down when Mac turned to look at her. Nimue's smirk mirrored Amber's in a moment of solidarity. Nice.

"Why?" Mac crouched down to meet her eyes. "What do you have planned?"

"Nothing. I know as much as you do, which is not much."

"I don't believe you."

"All I know is that when I try to remember, I can't. All I hear is this unmoored voice telling me what to do."

"A voice?" Amber asked.

"It's deep, unnerving, asking me to do things I don't want to. All the time. I ignored it so I could be with Zaraquel. I thought she was nice to me, and…well, we could be friends. I was wrong because you took me here."

She looked down and suddenly was overwhelmed with fear of what the Tall Dark Man would think or do if he knew where she was.

Shit. Will he retaliate?

"What? What is it?" Mac barked.

She flinched, her back hitting the metal of the chair.

"Hey, Nimue, what's wrong?" Amber reached out and placed her hand on her knee. Amber was hit with the memory Nimue was thinking of. She gasped and took a step back.

The Tall Dark Man. He towered over a meager Nimue stuck on her bed.

Mac leapt to his feet. "Amber, are you okay?"

She weakly shook her head, yes, and he lashed out at Nimue, "What did you do to her?"

"I...I...."

"Mac, relax. *She* didn't do anything. It was him."

"Him? Him who?" He looked back and forth between Amber and Nimue and waited for one of them to answer.

Finally, Nimue spoke up. "The Tall Dark Man."

The moment she said the words aloud, she knew what had to be done. Nimue felt it in her bones. Despite the tiny hairs on her arms that now stood at attention, she swallowed her fear and spoke in a childlike voice. That was how scared she was.

"Do the spell," she said, loud enough to project confidence, although, at that moment, all she felt was fear that crept up slowly, like bile in her throat.

"The Tall Dark Man?" Mac looked up incredulously and then addressed Amber. "Are you sure?"

She nodded. "Positive. I don't know how, but yeah. It's him."

"Shit, I don't know a spell strong enough. Rowe, he never...." His voice broke, and she wondered who this Rowe was. "He never taught me anything of that sort."

Nimue, nonetheless the willing volunteer, tried to make herself useful. She cleared her throat. "I may be of assistance."

"How so?" Amber asked out of pure curiosity.

"How can we trust you?" Mac raised a brow.

Enough. Nimue had had enough of her person being on trial as if she'd done something wrong. Must they forget that she was the victim here?

Jaw clenched and fists at her sides, she stood and, step by step, she walked out of the circle and broke the perimeter. A thin, iridescent veil was lifted as she walked toward them. Her eyes glowed with determination. She wanted to do this. She was ready.

"I want to know the truth as much as you do, if not more."

They assessed her, looking her straight in the eyes to see if she was lying. She wasn't. They knew this.

"All right," Mac sighed in defeat. "Tell me the spell."

Like the rest of her magic, Nimue couldn't explain how she knew this enchantment, but she did. She knew the words were right as they left her lips. "Since I am the party that the spell is being enacted on, I cannot say the words. It has to be you, both of you. Only then can it work."

They nodded in agreement, and she continued. "*Verum esto surge mendacium cernebatur. Solam veritatem.*"

Mac and Amber repeated the words over and over until Nimue floated in the air. She smiled down at them. It was working!

The world around her stilled, their words but a whisper, and a sudden ringing in her ears began. All Nimue saw was darkness. A pitch-black void just like before.

CHAPTER 6

Zaraquel

Pacing impatiently across her room, Zaraquel was desperate for any kind of update on Nimue. She grew more restless being cooped up in her room than when she was grounded as punishment.

An idea struck, Zaraquel could make a temporary copy of herself, just as Uncle Mac had taught her for distracting her enemy. Her parents weren't necessarily enemies, but they were close enough at the moment.

"*Duplex tribulatio.*" And in a blink of an eye, she was looking at her double. It looked like her, an exact replica. "Perfect." Zaraquel smiled at herself, and Z2 responded in kind. She gave her double the nickname Z2. It stuck.

"Now, Z2, you're gonna sit here and read some books, okay? Don't tell Mom or Dad anything. Got it?"

"Got it." Z2 winked and picked up a book as she waved

goodbye to Zaraquel, who flew out the window as soon as she got a chance.

Zaraquel only had a couple of hours to find Nimue and a lot of ground to cover.

"Shit," she muttered as she flew high above the Order's premises.

***

Nimue

Floating in the air with her eyes velvet black, Nimue was flooded with an overwhelming sensation. Her body vibrated, consumed by the power of the spell. Below, she heard the worried murmurs of Mac and Amber.

"Is that supposed to happen?"

"I don't know."

Their voices melded together until they sounded deep and slow, like molasses. The strength of the spell was immense. Nimue could feel the barrier falling away as the truth began to surface. She saw it all in a flash. Her body wavered in the air while her hands shook uncontrollably.

More voices.

"Is she okay?"

"I don't think she'll be able to answer our questions."

And then a deeper one stood out from the rest, *his* voice. *"You are disobeying me, Nimue. Stop."*

Her lips quivered as she tried to speak, her chest heaving as she tried to catch her breath. She willed herself to gain some semblance of control. "No."

With that single syllable of strength uttered, her eyes

shifted from black to white. They glowed like moonlight reflected on a lake. She heard gasps below, but she could not stop the purge from happening.

Before them on the walls of the dark dungeon and through her white gaze, she projected the truth of her life. All of her life was viewed as if she were seeing it for the first time. Each memory attacked her body with a jolt. She screamed.

A shock to the system.

"Camelot," she murmured.

She saw herself as she rose from the lake and bestowed Excalibur to King Arthur himself. She looked soft, shiny, and new, with her skin drenched in water in comparison to the rough exterior of the king. Behind him, however, stood a far more interesting figure hidden by a hood.

Jolt.

Once again, she saw herself in the middle of the woods with a man. She looked at how they interacted, and she felt somewhat at home with him, like he could understand her and give her what she wanted.

"Is that—?" Amber was cut off by Mac.

"It's Merlin."

At the sound of his name, she was hit with the significance of the vision. Nimue was playing with him. Of course, she was. That's what she did. She wanted to learn from him, but most importantly, she wanted to *be* him. She did not want to be considered less than him simply because of her female form. What Nimue desired was to be the only one that held that much power, and Merlin was standing in her way.

Another jolt. Her body moved as if guided by a drunken puppeteer.

The tunnel from whence she came was now in clear view. But it was vastly different from today's present tunnel. Rifling through the books and walking beside Merlin, she remembered feeling the magic.

It was warm, as if she were to get close enough. It'd heat her skin. The magic was alive. It was pure and vibrant and lived within the earth. And then Nimue's sight narrowed in on the amulet in Merlin's hands.

She heard his voice echo in her ears and thus reverberating through the room they were in. "This amulet contains the source of power needed to keep this 'living library' afloat."

Nimue saw the way her eyes glittered at the prospect of gaining so much magic. She saw the greed and the darkness that lived within her, and she did not like it one bit.

Jolt.

Again she saw them together. In the water and in each other's arms, their passion lit up the skies. Their attraction was out of this world. It appeared as if she loved him, the way they looked into each other's eyes with shared affection. That couldn't be fabricated — could it?

Nimue felt her limbs grow numb, the memories too strong for her control. Before she hit the ground, Mac and Amber were there to catch her. Her body felt heavy, and her eyes watered. Could she truly had been so deceitful? She couldn't bear to think of it, but she had to.

She had to discover who she was. The light began to

fade from her eyes, and her saviors shared a look of concern. "Let's take a break." Mac cleared his throat.

Nimue clutched onto his arm and frantically shook her head no. "Keep going. *Please.*"

She knew what he saw when he looked down at her, a desperate shell of a woman, and that's exactly how she felt. So, he took pity on her, and they recited the enchantment again.

In a quick succession of jolts, her eyes burst open as a sudden rush of her past was laid out there for them to see. In it, they saw the moment magic returned to the land; the betrayal as Nimue's past intentions were revealed with the amulet finally in her hands; the instant Merlin stripped her of her powers.

In their arms, Nimue was hit with a wave of anger, with a relented need for revenge. Having only felt this for the first time since she woke up, she didn't quite know what to make of it.

And that's when she saw him, the Tall Dark Man, not as how he usually revealed himself, but as a goat, the day she sealed her fate and sold her soul. Watching this being recounted before her very eyes, Nimue couldn't help but feel empty.

And she continued to relive the memories until they revealed every ounce of truth her despicable life held. For when she closed her eyes, she knew that when she opened them, Nimue would be held accountable for her past sins.

***

Zaraquel

"That light. Light. Where did it go?" she muttered to herself. Zaraquel had been following a bright light that appeared out of nowhere. It seemed pretty magical, so by her logic, she decided to go forth and follow it.

It flickered, however, until it completely stopped. A few moments ticked by until she saw the light again, and with great speed, she flew towards it.

Floating right above it, she stopped to catch her breath. She gently descended to the ground and found a latch. She opened the door and walked into the tunnel where the light burned bright.

***

Nimue

Body and mind wrecked from the truth spell, Nimue laid restlessly, turning on a bed. Given the havoc, she was rewarded with a place to sleep rather than just having her wounds nursed while on the floor. There were moments since she discovered her true nature that she awoke from her slumber just to scream and cry and mourn for the person she had thought she was. Nimue believed she was good, like Zaraquel, but it turned out she was nothing but a cheat, a fraud.

Sleep found her again, and she was attacked with the arrival of the Tall Dark Man in her dreams. His wispy shadow held Nimue in a tight grasp. "Nimue, it is your duty to lead Zaraquel onto the path of darkness. Do not forget that the angel is to be mine."

"N…n…," she uttered.

He held on tighter to her. "You are mine," he growled. "And given as you now remember who you truly are, you know what I can take away."

Her eyes widened in realization: *her power, her life.*

"Now, do it."

The Tall Dark Man released Nimue, and she fell, only to wake up gasping for breath in her waking life.

***

Zaraquel

With the bright light now gone, Zaraquel no longer had a guide. She heard someone cough furiously and walked faster since she did not want to lose the sound she was tailing. The coughs morphed into morose, long sobs. They got louder and louder as she reached an opening.

In a tiny sliver of moonlight cast down in the darkness, she spotted Nimue wrapped up in herself.

Shivers ran down her spine. *What did they do to her?*

Zaraquel cautiously approached her, and the moment her fingers made contact with Nimue's cold skin, Nimue sat up and backed away.

"Nimue?"

"S...stay away!"

Zaraquel looked at the Nimue before her and was reminded of the lost and scared soul that she first met. Her hair was disheveled, her lips chapped, and her eyes scanned the place like a scared cat. This wasn't the Nimue she knew.

"It's me, Zaraquel. Don't you remember me?"

Nimue violently shook her head. "Go away. L...leave

me!"

She moved closer and gathered Nimue in her arms. "C'mon, I'll take you somewhere safe. Somewhere warm, okay?"

Nimue was too tired and weak to resist, so she didn't and let Zaraquel guide her out. Their gazes met, and Zaraquel heard Nimue's faint whisper. "Why are you doing this?"

She responded with a sad smile, "Because you're my friend, Nimue."

"Friend?"

Zaraquel nodded as they continued to walk the way Zaraquel had come in. "But you're missing your friend?"

Her best friend. "Yes. Rae."

For a second, Zaraquel saw doubt in Nimue's eyes, but that was replaced with something she didn't recognize. Determination? Strength? She didn't know.

"I can help you get her back." Not wanting to alert them of their escape, Zaraquel wanted to scream with excitement but didn't. Instead, she settled for a hug. "Finally."

***

Nimue

"Do it. Do it."

The Tall Dark Man's threat grew stronger and stronger the further they got away from where she was kept prisoner. Held up by Zaraquel as they flew across the city, Nimue's mind was filled with an overload of memories, both good and bad, mostly bad.

She still couldn't wrap her head around the person

she'd seen projected in the cave. That was her. That *is* her. A woman capable of anything to attain power. That's all she had wanted but was that still what she wants?

But if the memories were all she had, did she have any other choice? Who was she *without* power? Without magic?

She shook her head from all the thoughts and stuck to the task at hand: the innocent.

Here's the thing about the innocents — their aura was different. It was white, and it glowed, but there was a certain shimmer that glittered when it hit the light. And there, above the cemetery, was a young woman placing flowers at a grave.

She pointed down to let Zaraquel know. "There. That girl right there, she's a good one."

"The one with the yellow coat?"

"Yes."

They made their slow descent and hid in the bushes as they observed their potential prey. The woman, it appeared, spoke to her mother as she sat on the damp ground.

"Hey Mom, I'm back." She laughed to herself and then sobered up when she found herself crying.

Nimue and Zaraquel shared a look.

"I'm ready." Zaraquel began to stand. She spoke with a newfound confidence that wasn't there when they first met. Nimue turned to look at her and was startled by what she saw. She'd seen that look: full of lust for power.

She herself had that look.

But what had that gotten her? Truly?

Her need for magic had only led to her own destruction.

She was alone.

Nimue couldn't and wouldn't do that to Zaraquel. She was so much better than her. Zaraquel was innately good. She was merely grieving. She missed her friend.

Nimue could understand loss—after all, she didn't know who she was and had only discovered hours ago. One thing she did know with all the certainty in her body was that she didn't want to be the Nimue she saw revealed via the spell.

Feeling a tear roll down her cheek, she wiped it away and took a breath.

She knew what she had to do. Reaching out, she took Zaraquel by the shoulder. "Stop."

"What? What are you talking about?"

"You can't do this, Zaraquel," Nimue pleaded. "You would never forgive yourself. Neither would I."

Zaraquel lashed out and pulled away from her grasp, "*You* can't do this! You promised. You said you would help me bring her back!"

Nimue grabbed her by the shoulders and tried to calm her down. "If we bring her back, she won't be the Rae you remember."

"W…what?" Zaraquel asked, her voice breaking from the emotions that took over.

"Once someone passes to the other side, a part of them stays there. And if returned, that said individual will always have a feeling something is missing. Like they're incomplete. Is that what you want for Rae? To have her constantly searching for a piece of her soul that she can never get back?"

"No. I don't want that."

"You have to let go, Z."

"It's too hard." She leaned in and hugged Nimue. "I don't want to forget her."

"You won't. Rae is a part of you, a part of your heart, and that's where she'll stay."

With Zaraquel in her arms, only Nimue could see that Chloe and Mac had found them. They approached but stopped when they heard Zaraquel struggling to form words as she cried.

The girls parted, and Zaraquel stood there still, rendered immobile, the shock finally settling into her system. "Oh my God, Nimue. I would have done it. I would have killed her."

"But you didn't," Nimue reasoned proudly.

Zaraquel's eyes shone with appreciation. "Because of you, I didn't."

Behind her, she saw the look of shock from both Chloe and Mac. But Nimue shook her head in disagreement. "You chose not to follow through when you very well could've."

"Is that true?" Chloe asked.

Zaraquel whipped around at the sound of her mother's voice. "Mom?" She ran over to her mother's arms, and Nimue looked over at them fondly. Mac caught this, and they shared a look of acceptance towards one another.

"Let's go home, ladies," Mac said as he began to walk off. "*All* of us."

Zaraquel turned and smiled brightly at Nimue and then back at her mother. With hurried steps, Nimue began to walk into her new life. But it was as if the wind was knocked out of her, and she froze, her hand clutching her stomach.

The wind picked up, and her skin prickled with gooseflesh. *He's here. The Tall Dark Man is here.*

As if he were standing right behind her, he growled, "You threw everything I gave you away, you insolent child! You betrayed *me,* and you shall pay the ultimate price."

Piercing her chest, she felt a hand grip her heart with a heavy *whoosh!* She felt weak at the knees. She lost her balance and fell to the ground. Clutching her heart, she realized that he'd taken something from her. Something that made her special.

"You no longer have what you treasure most, eternal life. You're mortal, dear, and as such, your death is imminent."

Imminent.

Imminent.

Imminent.

As the last word echoed in her ears, the Tall Dark Man granted her one last gift: her vision of her death. She would die as she had arrived on this earth by water; she just didn't know when.

"Nimue?" Zaraquel's voice shattered the silence, and Nimue looked up to see the hope in her eyes. "You coming?"

With her head held high, Nimue regained her composure and smiled, her feet slowly unsticking from the ground that held her. "Just a moment."

And perhaps that was all she had, a moment. But if that were true, Nimue wanted to spend her time undoing all the evil she'd done in her past. She had to—this was her second and last chance.

CHAPTER 7

Zaraquel

It had been a few months since that frightful night when she almost took an innocent life. Zaraquel sat upon the roof night after night, the guilt built up in the pit of her stomach. With her wings wrapped against her body, she felt small. Too small for her liking.

Had Nimue not stepped in, she would've gone through with it. Come to think of it, she would have done anything to get Rae back. But the cosmos had a plan when they brought Nimue onto her path.

Nimue was her saving grace. And for that, she was grateful, then, now, and in the future, for as long as they were friends. Nonetheless, the knowledge of having her friend by her side didn't assuage the remorse she felt. She doubted every move she made, every flick of her hand, or spell she cast.

Her misgivings swirled in her head. And simply put, Zaraquel's confidence was gone.

Moreover, since that night, where her fate hung in the balance, Zaraquel had noticed something strange happening to her. It started as a tingling sensation on the tips of her wings, which she shrugged off as growing pains. But then, just as that started, it stopped days later. She lost track of time, hours at times and woke up with no knowledge of the time that had passed.

Her body was trying to tell her something, of that Zaraquel was certain, but she didn't know what.

Was this her punishment? To live in a state of constant uncertainty?

She didn't know, and she was scared to find out.

**

Nimue

Having been shown her death by the Tall Dark Man months ago, that vision haunted her dreams every night. Although she had yet to get a good night's sleep, Nimue was determined not to let that get to her. She had weathered worse. She was here, and she was alive, for whatever time she had left, and she would use it accordingly.

Her present was her own.

Nimue felt at home in The Order. A new sense of purpose had filled her soul—saving and helping others was her new goal. The grounds of The Order brimmed with magic—she felt it in her bones, yet she didn't feel the need to take it for herself as she once did in her past life. With her memories no longer scrambled, her knowledge was abundant. She knew that, and so did Mac. Nimue was fully aware that he wanted to see her limits if any.

Something light and airy bubbled in her chest, something like happiness.

Is this what happiness feels like?

Her hands shook with nervous energy as she mentally ran down today's lesson plan. The blades of grass pricked her bare feet as she paced back and forth.

I can do this.

After extensive training and evaluating to see if dark magic was still pervading her motives, it wasn't, and Nimue passed with flying colors. She was ready to teach others what she had learned in all her years on this earth.

Today was the day.

Her thoughts are interrupted when she heard Mac clear his throat, and her eyes sprung open, her embarrassment evident on her cheeks.

"Am I interrupting?" Mac quirked a small smile.

This was new, their repartee. Nimue could tell that Mac remained a bit apprehensive. He'd stare at her as if he was still trying to figure her out.

He was doing that currently, now with a smirk.

"Uh no, just going through the lesson," she pointed to her right temple, "in my head."

"Right." His hands were laced behind his back as the group of children quietly giggled in the background.

She broke eye contact with Mac and met the children with a warm smile. "All right, kids, let's make a circle and sit down so our first lesson can begin."

They quickly ran and assumed their spots, all excited to learn magic. Meanwhile, Mac lingered, his back against a tree, shadowing her lesson.

Of course, Nimue was there under a provisional status—her next three months in constant supervision from The Order's elders, Mac, Chloe, Amber, and Malakai.

She took a seat in the center of the circle and inhaled a deep breath. "Now, in order to understand magic and how it works, we must learn to appreciate where it comes from...."

***

Zaraquel

While on her way to meet Nimue for lunch, Zaraquel managed a long stroll to the clearing. She liked the tranquility nature brought her. It was quiet, save for the billowing wind and rustling of the swaying trees.

She took a moment to spin around in a circle, just needing a breather. Her laughter drowned out her fears. Zaraquel stopped and clumsily slumped to the ground, her hair splayed beneath her. At that precise moment, a butterfly landed on the tip of her nose. She marveled at the iridescent and translucent quality of its wings.

"Wow."

Only seconds later, Zaraquel realized the butterfly had stopped fluttering its wings like something or someone was sucking the life out of it. As a result, the color drained from its being. A butterfly in shades of gray fell to the ground beside her.

Freaked, she quickly stood and gasped. "What the hell?"

Her feet sprung from the grass and into the air as she unfurled her wings and floated above where she had been lying. There, beneath her, was her silhouette imprinted on the grass, lifeless, just like the butterfly.

"What is going on?" She looked at her hands in fear as her voice cracked. "What is happening to me?"

"Zaraquel!" From a distance, she heard Nimue calling to her.

Perhaps Nimue will know, she thought to herself.

Zaraquel sincerely hoped she did.

***

Nimue

Clutching onto the picnic basket filled with food, courtesy of Chloe, Nimue called out to her friend.

"Zaraquel! Zaraquel, where are you?"

How strange. She's usually punctual, especially when it comes to food.

Nimue continued to walk through the woods until she felt a ferocious wind hurling in her direction. She shielded her eyes but caught a glimpse of Zaraquel as she halted abruptly before her.

"Zaraquel?" Nimue questioned. "What's wrong?" She placed the picnic basket on the ground. Nimue reached out her hand to comfort her, but Zaraquel quickly backed away, checking over her shoulder, leery of touching anything or anyone, it seemed. Nimue took a few cautious steps towards her. She repeated, "What's wrong, Z?"

"I…I don't know." Zaraquel's voice was shaky.

"Okay." Nimue steadied her tone. "That's okay. Walk me through it, all right? Let's talk it out, yeah? Sit down. You need to eat something."

With a snap of her fingers, the picnic spread was perfectly laid out.

Zaraquel nodded and described the changes that had taken a toll on her body as she munched on a piece of bread.

Poor Z.

Nimue processed this new information and popped a grape into her mouth. "Sounds like you have a new power."

Taken aback, Zaraquel stopped eating. "What? Is that even possible?"

"It's rare but certainly possible."

"Great. Just add it to the list," Zaraquel muttered sarcastically.

"What list?"

"Of the weird things about me."

"Listen, you are *not* weird. You're special—there's a difference."

Zaraquel rolled her eyes. "You sound like my mom."

"Good. She's a smart woman," Nimue smirked.

"Whatever," Zaraquel huffed. "Can we fix it?"

Nimue tilted her head, oblivious to the concern. "Fix it? Why would you want to fix it when you can learn to control it?"

"C…can I control it? I mean, it just sprouted out of nowhere. Like a zit."

Nimue couldn't help but laugh as she composed herself. "Remember, the only thing that's not in our power to control is…." Nimue waited for Zaraquel to answer.

"Death," she somberly responded. "I know, Nimue."

Not happy with seeing her little friend sad, Nimue recalled the legend of a totem that could help Zaraquel on her journey. A smile reached her face as she remembered where she last placed the amulet. It held such great power, perhaps it could help Zaraquel. She didn't know, but she wanted to give it a shot. Nimue tried to play off her worry for this growing new ability, but it was alarming. She needed to confide in the elders at once, not just for Zaraquel's safety but for The Order's as well.

It was Nimue's turn to save the world.

Nimue sat amongst the elders of The Order and told them about this totem that could help Zaraquel with her new power. She even told them about a feeling she was having that things were not quite over for them. Perhaps due to the latest dreams she was having and realizing that trust was earned from both sides, she came forward to her new family — at least that's what they meant to her now — and shared with them the dreams that kept her from sleeping peacefully.

She felt they were all ready to hear her worries. "See, I go to sleep with Z, and everything is good for a while. But then, I still hear his voice. It's not as loud as before, but it's more like a whisper. At least I think it is him, but I can't be sure. I thought the Tall Dark Man would've left me alone by now.

"Once I get to a certain point in my sleep, it starts. I

picture this vampire, but I don't recognize him. I hear the Tall Dark Man whispering to him and running his hand up and down his cheek like he's feeding him evil thoughts. Know what I'm saying? I know he's a vampire because I feel it. I don't know how, but I feel it. I can't see his face because it's darkened somehow. It looks like he is slumped over, with no life left in him, but he is still alive. I see everything. I see the man once in a while try to break free from the chains that bind him, but he can't. The Tall Dark Man whispers to him, in his face, 'You will serve me soon, sweet boy. I will have you rise and become unstoppable. Not only will you be a hunter, but you will also be a vampire and more. There will be no stopping you.'"

Nimue continued to describe the rest of her dream, but looking at Amber, Malakai, Mac, and Chloe, she wasn't sure they were ready to hear any more. Amber broke the silence. "We know it couldn't be Michael—his head was severed from his body. It isn't possible. But what about Valentine? Could he be brought back?"

Nimue nodded in disagreement. She couldn't tell if it was someone they knew or someone yet to meet. She felt their pain and knew she wanted to help them. She closed her eyes and began to speak a chant. When she opened her eyes, she began to tell them more.

"I have asked the Mother Earth, the most powerful source of magic there is, to guide you when the time comes, and if you are worthy, you will one day know who the Tall Dark Man has in his power. Till then, Mother Earth said simply, 'Prepare and guard the side of truth and justice. The

Prophecy is not yet complete.' I don't know what that all means, but consider me a messenger for you to help you."

This time Mac spoke up. "If this is someone the Tall Dark Man is sending, then the worst is yet to come. Have you and Marcus considered searching the estate for additional sources of wisdom? Perhaps I could speak with Marcus and see if there is a way to contact Kabos. Apparently, ghost or not, he has information we need if we are to prepare for something we don't know is coming. Let's pack up and leave for the estate at once. Preparations are needed, and we need this time not only for ourselves but to ready Zaraquel for whatever power has been given to her. And you, Amber, need to do the hardest task of all. You and Marcus must go through all of Michael's possessions and see what he has that we do not know about. While it has only been months, we need to see if there was anything he left behind."

Everyone nodded in agreement and prepared to head back to the estate. Preparations for the worst to come had to start, and with heavy hearts, they went back to the place they kept sacred so they would not lose their precious memories of Michael before he changed. Nimue felt at peace knowing she was going to go with them and help them with their preparations, all while dreading another possible battle with the Tall Dark Man. Deep down, she wondered what it would take to make him stop.

CHAPTER 8

Amber

As they arrived at the estate, Amber suddenly felt anxious to set foot back inside, but she knew that before he changed, Michael had truly loved her and all their friends. She kept reminding herself that he was a pawn, like so many others, used for the simple purpose of trying to kill her and stop the prophecy.

Marcus must've heard them approaching because Amber saw him running from the mansion, calling to them. She smiled, and she knew that Zaraquel and Chloe needed time alone with him to be a family. Once all the hugging was over with, Amber took Nimue by the hand and led her to the front.

"Marcus, I believe we all were never properly introduced to Nimue. Before you bare your fangs, she's been through a lot. We all have recently. Is everything the same, or did you already make changes?" she said jokingly while giving him a nudge in the shoulder that left him flying backwards since she used her strength.

Marcus yelled from across the way, "Geez, Amber, give a vamp a little break! I didn't change much. Just put your room in the basement!"

Laughing and joking like old times helped make this easier until she saw Jerome come out with snacks. "Queen Amber, this old man has missed you terribly. May I offer some refreshments or anything? Welcome back to all of you! There are matters to attend to as well."

Amber and the gang entered the house and found that things were all the same.

***

Zaraquel

"Dad! Did you touch anything in my room? I want to show it to Nimue, and...well, I hope you don't mind, but I'm gonna share my room with her. She's not Rae, but she's just as important to me as she was."

She reached for Nimue's hand, and both ran up the stairs and into her room. The girls were giggling up a storm and unpacking at the same time. Zaraquel motioned for Nimue to look under what was Rae's bed and showed her the loose floorboards. Nimue looked at her with a questioning face, but Zaraquel put her fingers over her lips and made the motion to be quiet. She pried open the floorboard and pulled out a small box. Rae loved to have secret places in the floorboards at the Order and at the estate. It drove her nuts, but it was fun to hide surprises for her.

"This was Rae's. She told me to open it only if something happened to her. I feel better about opening it with you here. Are you ready?"

Nimue nodded and appeared to be fixated with the box, as her eyes never left it.

"What is it? What do you see?"

"Z, don't tell me you don't see it? There's a design on it, but it is faded. The box looks rather old. Like really old."

Zaraquel stared at the box more closely, and there she saw a design covered by dust. Using her sleeve, she rubbed at it and saw it—the witches' symbol that was in the witches' books regarding spells and the prophecy. There was no lock, just a little latch. Flipping the latch, she lifted the lid to the box. Inside lay a small parchment rolled and tied with a ribbon. Taking it out, she untied the ribbon and opened it to read out loud.

"Death Magic. To reach the soul that you seek, chant the words before, during, and after lighting a white candle. You must add the name of the spirit you wish to seek at the end. Repeat a total of three times. Then wave a sprig of rosemary over the flame to prevent the evil spirits from entering your world. This spell opens the doorway to let the spirit you want to cross over for twenty-four hours only. Once they have crossed, the doorway will remain open, so the rosemary must remain over the flame for the twenty-four hours. Take heed in using this spell, for it can't be used lightly. All spirits, those pure or unpure, will seek to cross.

"Loqueris ad me in spiritu perierat requiram."

Zaraquel couldn't believe it! She had a way to bring back Rae, if only for twenty-four hours. But, remembering what Nimue told her, there was always a cost. What would this spell cost? She handed the parchment to Nimue and looked in the box to see if there was more. And there was. A handwritten note in Rae's writing.

My best friend. If you are reading this, you will know that I am dead. There, I said it. Dead to you, to the world, and most of all, to Chloe. I put this letter in with the one spell I took from the coven the last time we were there. I was afraid I would lose cousin Chloe and wanted a way to save her. But if you have found this, then I am the one you want to save. I remembered from my mom that there is a price to pay to bring me back. I found more information in the books in the library. It's with Chloe's books on the Witches' Prophecy. The spell was written by Tituba, one of Satan's many consorts. Be careful, my friend, and I pray that one day I can return to you and the others. And if not, my death was not in vain. I was young, I am half-demon, and to bring me back may not be all that you seek, for the acheri side will want vengeance. But I learned from Chloe that that may not always be the answer. I will watch over you, but do you really need it, Zaraquel? Love Always and Forever, Rae

Zaraquel wiped away a tear and looked at the note once more. "I have it, Nimue! We can bring her back, but only for a short time. But, if we search through my mom's books, we may be able to find a more powerful spell. Should we try it?"

Nimue shrugged and remained silent.

"Nimue, tell me. You are more powerful than me, but together we might be able to save Rae."

"I think this is more than dark magic. I think this is a lot worse, and it might be dangerous. Should we talk to McPherson and Amber? I gave them my word to listen and behave in order to stay here with you all."

Zaraquel thought about it, then she raised her hand, palm facing toward Nimue, and called forth a force that knocked Nimue backwards. Nimue returned the gesture in kind, but Zaraquel was able to dodge it by opening her wings and flying towards the ceiling. Zaraquel didn't want to fight her new friend, but no one seemed to understand how much she missed Rae. How much she needed her back.

Finally, Nimue lowered her hand, hung her head, and relented. "I know how you feel. I would love to see you happy again. Let's try. Do we have someplace safe here we can do the spell without everyone knowing?"

Zaraquel was happy to hear those words and nodded. "Rae and I would practice at night while the house was asleep. I would cast a silence spell so no one would hear us. We can try tonight."

Zaraquel came down and hugged her new friend. Maybe there was hope yet.

CHAPTER 9

Zaraquel

It was around midnight when Zaraquel opened her eyes. She climbed out of bed and woke Nimue. Earlier that evening, they had managed to sneak around and find the items the spell called for. Placing a blanket in the center of the room, both girls sat down, and Zaraquel cast the silence spell. Then, opening the parchment, both girls held hands and chanted according to the directions. The flame flickered and changed color as the smell of rosemary filled the room. Chills ran up and down both girls' arms, and Zaraquel noticed the hairs on both rising. Watching the flame again, they chanted the final round, and as they said the last word, the rosemary rose from her hand and sat directly above the flame on its own. It would stay in place if the flame continued to stay lit. The white candle was now black, a sign of the Death Magic. There was no other sound in the room. Finally, smoke rose from the flame and thickened.

A hole opened in the smoke, and there appeared Rae. She was smiling.

Nimue spoke. "Is that you, Rae? I warn you that I am no stranger to this, and you will not harm Zaraquel."

Zaraquel couldn't find the words right away, but she managed to tell Nimue that this was Rae.

The figure of Rae became more defined in the smoke. "I am Rae. I miss you, Z."

Gathering up the courage, Zaraquel begged the spirit to tell her how to bring her back. "I can't live without you, Rae. I know there will be a price, but if there is a way without taking a life, I would do anything to try. I can't be here without you. Oh, this is Nimue. She used to be bad on the side of the Tall Dark Man, but we are her family now."

The spirit smiled. "If you managed to do this, then there is another way. Another way is without taking a life, but there will be an imbalance in the world. This is Death Magic, old, powerful, and dark. You would have to study the art of dark magic and become the balance of light and dark magic. This will require time and patience, Z. It will not come easily. Not even Chloe managed the balance. You are going to need more than one teacher. McPherson can't teach you the dark magic or death magic. You will need an ancient witch, a powerful trinket from both sides of magic, and here is the hard part. You will need to find another demon witch. Someone like me would probably be best, but my witch half was always stronger. This time you need someone more demon like, and I don't know if Amber or Chloe are going to like this. If you use the Seek the Demon spell in one of Chloe's books, you will release your request to the demon world. They will seek you out, which can be dangerous. Are you sure you want this, Z? I'm getting scared talking about it."

After she thought about this for a moment, Zaraquel found the words. "I need you. I need both you and Nimue. I can't explain it, but I feel there is something coming for me. I will do anything, but like Nimue taught me, I can't do the killing like that. Remember, I can only do justified kills. But I will learn. What else can you tell me? What's it like where you are? Where are you exactly?"

The spirit floated closer to the girls.

"Nimue, ever hear of the Totem of Death? Zaraquel will need that to wield the power of necromancy. We were subjected to necromancy before the battle, but that was without balance. We also need the Totem of Life before you try to bring me back. Seek these totems, learn what you can, and find the balance. I am between life and death right now because it can't be determined where I will rest. In fact, I kinda have been avoiding the pit and the light. I think I like spying on all the dead demons and stuff. But I can go to either side. Nimue, have you really left the Tall Dark Man? You better not hurt my friends, or I will haunt you forever."

Nimue smiled. "I would never hurt them. They helped me to remember, and now, I know I must help them to save the world if that ever happens again. I can't let the Tall Dark Man win."

The spirit of Rae smiled and nodded. She was here for twenty-four hours, and the girls were getting tired. Zaraquel was yawning and started drifting to sleep. But she could hear Nimue and Rae talking about magic and the things they knew she had yet to learn.

When morning came, the flame was still glowing. Nimue must've been up all night talking to Rae. Both started talking to her once they saw her eyes open.

"Shh, I'm just waking up. Let me get my notebook for the list of things we need to do."

Zaraquel started writing as Nimue, and the spirit of Rae provided her the list of items. It was definitely a long list. Finally, Zaraquel spoke.

"Okay, let me try out my new power and see if I can leave my body again and look through my mom's books. It's the only way to go through them. She gets so uptight if I am looking at her books to practice."

With that, Zaraquel left her body and the room and floated through the house to search through Chloe's books. No one was awake yet. She used the craft to flip open the books, and once she found a few that might be useful, she made herself memorize them. After a few more minutes, her power was fading, and she found herself back in her body once she opened her eyes.

"Z, that was so cool. I can't believe you got a new power and I'm not there. This is not fair. Promise me that you will make me come back. I can't stand it that I miss you so much."

Zaraquel started to stand up but felt weak and collapsed. Nimue caught her, but the girls made a lot of noise. Luckily, the silence spell was still working.

***

Nimue

Nimue waited patiently, but she managed to speak to the spirit of Rae. She could tell that the spirit was friendly but very careful in its responses to her questions. The spirit motioned for Nimue to sit, and she obliged. Zaraquel lay on the floor, completely passed out from sheer exhaustion.

"Nimue, listen closely to me. There is not a lot of time, and this will be hard for Zaraquel to hear because of our friendship. The magic of the Order — you destroyed it, remember? But I know they rebuilt it to save it. In its depths lies a secret known only to Merlin, but surely he must have shared that knowledge with you during his teachings. There is a spell of old that will fortify a weapon forged in great heat, cooled in the coldest of ice. Surely you know what I am talking about. Say you do."

"I think I remember. But it is an ancient spell known only to those who call themselves gods. It didn't matter which gods, but they hold dominion over the elements considering all areas of faith. I do remember learning it, though, and it takes someone with immense power. That is not me, not now, not after what the Tall Dark Man did to me. But I can teach someone, with power, the spell. But that's not it, is it? There's more you are not saying."

The spirit of Rae smiled but remained silent. It looked like she was hanging her head low out of desperation, but Nimue wasn't quite sure.

"The spell is not the only thing, and neither is bringing me back, as much as I'd like to be back. It's creepy here. I heard the demons and all the other evil things here talking. They think I'm not a threat because I'm a half demon and already dead. The Tall Dark Man said the ancient prophecy is holding true. There are three battles, not just one. The one that was just fought was the second. The third is more…I guess you could say it would be the end of the world and does not require the queen's blood or anything. He is creating a more powerful servant that he will unleash somehow. He plans to have Zaraquel as his angel. An angel of the dark side. The weapon, the totems I told you about, the magic, are just the beginning. The family will need to prepare like never before. I am wise beyond my years, thanks to my acheri side. You must help them research and prepare if you truly plan to redeem yourself, or you will never have your soul back entirely. Part of you still belongs to him, and he is holding onto you for when it is time to wake that part of you up to serve him again. He is just letting you think you are free. Do not get comfortable, for this is just the beginning."

Nimue shuddered, but she knew the spirit did not lie to her. She sensed his presence in the back of her mind, but it lay dormant. Closing her eyes, she took a deep breath and began to chant a calming spell. Her soul was in turmoil, and she didn't even know it. Parts of her memory recalled the old spell and the totem she knew she had hidden to keep it safe, but as for the other two totems, life and death, those would have to be searched for, like treasure. It was time for a treasure hunt, but where to begin?

Nimue tried to wake Zaraquel so that she could share the news of what she just learned.

CHAPTER 10

Zaraquel

Zaraquel listened to the news and looked at the spirit. It was soon approaching the time where Rae would be gone again. This only strengthened her resolve to do all that was necessary to bring Rae back. But the first thing she realized the girls needed to do was to tell everyone, and Nimue had to come clean with all she'd learned. Before Rae disappeared, she gave her an air hug in hopes that Rae understood what she was going to do.

"I'm going to bring you back, Rae. Wait and see. I love you."

And then Rae vanished once more.

Zaraquel waited till everyone was up and having breakfast. Both she and Nimue took turns telling all that they had done and learned, knowing there would be some repercussions about doing things without supervision. Her mother gave her the look, and Zaraquel busted into tears.

"None of you thought how much I miss Rae. I have a new friend in Nimue, and she has prepared to help me. All you guys do is tell me what I can and can't do, rather than looking at me for ME! I'm not your average kid. I have wings, I fly, I do magic, I lost my best friend to YOUR battle, not mine. And now I have a chance to bring her back and more. Did you even think, Mom, Dad, that there is more to my part in this prophecy than just helping Auntie Amber?"

Nimue placed her hand on Zaraquel's shoulder and whispered to her. "I will help you. You are my best friend, even if I am not yours yet."

Zaraquel smiled at her and looked up at the adults. Even McPherson had a tear rolling down his cheek. He seemed to understand. He took the adults into a different room, leaving the two girls behind. Moments later, they all returned.

McPherson took control of the situation. "I think I understand what you are both saying. First, let's be clear. The battle is not over. It is as we feared. We will have peace, but we don't know for how long, so let's enjoy that part. Zara, your parents, Auntie Amber, and I talked. We see the journey you are facing. Well, the journey that is both yours and Nimue's. It will test the bounds of the moral compass in each of you. It will require work, patience, and listening, but it is not a journey you can do on your own. That is forbidden, especially with the Tall Dark Man having a hold on Nimue's soul. It will be dangerous. Are you both ready for that?"

Zaraquel and Nimue looked at each other and nodded. They knew there was so much work ahead for them to bring back Rae.

"You both need to realize that this path will also take time. It will not be done in a month—it may take years before you are ready to bring back Rae. Are you prepared to wait however long it takes to bring Rae back without taking an innocent life?"

"I am. She is, was, my best friend. I know in my heart of hearts that I truly need her to be complete, to fulfill whatever my destiny still holds for me. I know I am not done. None of us are."

McPherson stopped and looked at Marcus. This time Marcus spoke.

"Then, my beautiful, sweet angel of a daughter. No father or mother could ever be as proud of a daughter as we are. You and Nimue must go on this journey with McPherson. He is to be your teacher, your guide. You cannot go alone. We bid you leave to seek out what you need to find and return to us. While you are on your journey, Chloe, Amber, and I will have our own journey to prepare for the day that is yet to come. Is that a fair trade?"

Zaraquel ran to her parents and gave them a hug with her wings spread. Tears were shed, and the group came together. They would spend the next several days as a family all together, including Amber and Malakai, before McPherson took the girls on their journey that would find the answers they sought.

The day finally approached. Zaraquel and Nimue were packed and ready to go. Heartfelt wishes were said, hugs and kisses were shared, and the duo went off to meet McPherson at the Order. He told them it would be best for them all to have this family time while he prepared the items they would need.

The girls made their way to the Order and found McPherson ready to go. He managed to pack the SUV, and Zaraquel said, "It looks like we are going camping. Are you sure we are doing the right thing? I'm trying not to be scared, but this is all surreal."

Nimue clasped her hand and held it tight. Zaraquel could feel the reassurance radiate through her body and into the very tips of her wings. In return, she squeezed Nimue's hand as they made their way to the SUV and loaded up their backpacks.

"Hey, Uncle Mac, where are we going to go? Is it camping?" Zaraquel was always curious about everything.

Jokingly, McPherson said, "Yes, we are going to go snow camping! I know how much you love the cold weather!"

"You're teasing. Seriously, where are we going first? I mean, this journey isn't supposed to be easy if we've got to learn the darkest of all magic and stuff to bring back Rae, right?"

"Sweet Zaraquel. You and Nimue first must begin some magic training, but not the dark arts yet. First, we need to get you two to balance the power you have. You will find some of the Order's most powerful books in the back. While I drive to where we are going, why don't you two start looking through them and begin memorizing some of the key points in these books? Training will not be easy, but it is up to me as your teacher to prepare you. The others will have their own training with the help of some others, but we need not concern ourselves with that. You must focus on you throughout this entire journey.

"We will make many stops in many places. We will be guests at the places we stay. We will connect with nature, and we will have other teachers. So, you both promise me that from the minute we drive away, you are students. You are not the teachers. You must learn, practice, and breathe what you will learn. Agreed?"

Zaraquel realized the demands that were being asked of her and looked at Nimue. Nimue gave her a nod. In return, she said, "Yes, we promise. We are students. But, there better be a little fun too."

McPherson just smiled and finished loading the SUV before turning on the ignition. The girls hopped in, and the journey was underway. Zaraquel nicknamed them "The Travelers" and decided to make the most of this. A few hours into the ride, she couldn't take it any longer. Nimue was sleeping, and McPherson just kept driving.

"Where exactly are we going?"

"Z, aren't you a nosey thing? If I recall, you must learn dark magic. We are going to find you a teacher of the dark arts. Someone I think we can trust — after all, you aren't a normal teen. They would have to understand that there must be a balance for you. If we choose the wrong teacher, you might lose the light magic within you."

Zaraquel gulped at that thought. She knew it wasn't going to be easy, but maybe this might not be a good idea. She didn't want to lose her angelic abilities or her magic. Her mother and father would be disappointed in her. And then there was the disappointment of Auntie Amber. As the drive continued, she was getting tired and decided to lay back just like Nimue and dream of Rae. She missed Rae so much.

CHAPTER 11

McPherson

Looking into the rearview mirror, he noticed that the girls were sleeping. He turned up the radio volume slightly so the girls would not hear him chant. Part of his training from Sebastian Rowe had included communicating with the spirits that secretly guarded the Order, a secret he kept to himself and did not share with the others for simple reasons. He feared that this knowledge might destroy their paths because as much as he knew about Kabos's part of the prophecy, Rowe also had his and had made sure that if anything happened to him, McPherson would be prepared. Once the chant was complete, a figure appeared in the passenger seat. In his heart, he wished it would have been Rowe, but it wasn't.

"Spirit of the heart, I called upon you to seek guidance in giving me the strength I will need for this quest. It is not my quest, but I am the teacher of the ones who must travel this road."

The spirit nodded as it turned to face Zaraquel and Nimue. "Seek out the witch of black. To find her, go back to the beginning of the witches. She has been reborn from the burnings. You will know her by the birthright on her wrist. Once you find her, you must let the young ones be. It will be up to them to master the balance and wield it or be destroyed. Your path lies elsewhere once they begin their path. For you, what you seek is far away. You will begin when the guides feel you are ready."

And with that knowledge, the spirit vanished, leaving McPherson alone in the front of the SUV. For hours he pondered over the spirit's guiding message, and with a heavy heart, he knew he would have to leave the girls alone, but he couldn't bring himself to do it. Perhaps it would be easier once he found their teacher. All he remembered was that the teacher was branded with something on her wrist. He needed to make a call but hoped the girls would remain sleeping so they would not hear.

He dialed Miriam's number. He hoped with her new connections as the Counselor for the Order, she would be able to tap into something to help him.

"Miriam? It's Mac. I could sure use your help about now. I have Zaraquel and Nimue. Both are asleep right now, but I think I am taking them on a very wild journey that none of us are really prepared for."

"Tell me all that has happened, but not before you at least tell me that Amber is safe."

"She is safe. She is preparing for…I know this sounds

weird. But there is supposed to be something coming with the prophecy. She is training for it. But right now, Zara needs and wants to bring back Rae, and there is supposed to be a dark magic teacher that we need to find. I have it on good faith that this teacher will have a birthmark that we can recognize, but she will have to balance both light and dark magic to succeed, something not even Chloe has mastered. Do you know of any texts in the Order that speak of bringing back someone from the dead with this?"

"I was just looking at something like that. Hold on. I think I have it right here. I needed to know about the history of the Order and came across it just this morning. Here it is. Let me thumb through it, and while I do, fill me in with more detail, please."

Mac took a deep breath and began to fill her in while he heard the rumbling of pages.

Miriam interrupted him. "I found it. It is written like this: There is one witch that it seems might fit the description, though there is not much history on her at all. Anne Koldings was believed to be a powerful witch from the 1590s in Denmark. It is said that she was called the 'mother of the devil' because of her ability to birth creatures from hell. Another legend has it that she would birth vampires in her garden, turning her roses to red. Of course, it is speculation on that part. But because many claimed that she could birth these creatures and she was known to birth something not human, she was feared until she was tortured to death. However, it is written that she told her executioner that she would return to life as promised by the devil himself and that her identity would never be discovered until she was truly needed by a pure soul. She cursed the executioner by claiming the life of his wife while she was in childbirth. She was burned after confessing to priests and a few others, but once the fire was out, there were no signs that she was even at the stake. The executioner was under scrutiny for some time.

"There's more. It is said that she was the most feared of all witches in Europe and that through her lying with the devil, many spawns were created, and they, in turn, do their bidding. She also lay with him when he was in the shape of a dog or goat, never a man. There is another part of the story that links her to the Hexham line of witches that have all birthed his children. They are no relation to each other but to the one we call the Tall Dark Man, also known as the devil himself. There is another book here that tries to outline the history of the Tall Dark Man, and it seems that Rowe kept adding to it as we all learned more about him. Even the parts I know involving my time with him are in here. It is all recorded. Shall I send you a copy of the book?"

Gulping deep at what he'd just listened to, Mac replied, "Does she have a birthmark or anything? Is there any record of that?"

He listened once more as Miriam flipped through pages and shuffled books around. She was certainly skimming through books in a hurry, by the sounds of it.

"Here. In another one of Rowe's books, more like a journal, he wrote that on the inside of her wrist, she bears the mark of the devil. More like a branding burned into her flesh. He drew a picture, and it is like my branding when I was held by him. You know what my branding looks like, right? Well, she supposedly has the same one."

"This is not good. If she were to teach the dark arts to the girls, how do we keep Zaraquel and Nimue safe? Thanks, Miriam. Do we know where she might be?"

"According to this, no. But there is a spell to call her, and she is bound to appear. It was how he had his hold on his witches. I will send you the spell through a secure message. Give me twenty minutes, and you will have it. Check your phone. Let me know if you need anything else and good luck to you all."

The call disconnected, and McPherson continued to drive until he could stop and check his message. Checking the rearview mirror, the girls were still asleep.

Finally, McPherson pulled into an all-night restaurant and woke the girls up. It was time they took a small break, had a meal, and did some talking. He had to have the girls ready for what was to come.

"Let's go inside, use the facilities, and order food. Zaraquel, make sure those wings stay hidden."

"Yes, Uncle Mac. Come on, Nimue, I will race you to the bathroom. Loser must sleep on the floor tonight."

He laughed as the girls took off, and he went to get a table. He looked through the menu while he waited for the girls. Though they may be different in years than the average human, they gave the appearance of teenage girls through every attitude, sassiness, and more. He shook his head at the mere thought, *This is what it is like to have teenage daughters.*

Finally, after what seemed like an eternity, the

girls found their way to the table and opened their menus. Zaraquel wanted the burger while Nimue ordered a simple salad. McPherson ordered coffee, eggs, bacon, and toast. He could never drive after eating a heavy meal.

While they waited for the server to bring the food, he began to tell them everything he'd learned from Miriam and from the spirit. He explained how he would have to leave them while they were being taught but would be reunited with them when the teaching was done. It would be impossible for him to stay with them and be in the vicinity of the dark magic.

"Zaraquel, I must stress how important the resistance to being tempted by the dark magic is. If this Anne Koldings is the teacher you need, she is the most feared of all the dark witches. Think of how your mom is loved by all the light witches. This will be the same, but in the opposite manner, with Anne Koldings. I need to make sure you girls hold dear, do not reveal, do not show your true intentions to this witch teacher. You need her, but I don't think she will be swayed to join our fight, our side, so don't bother trying. Just learn the dark arts from her and fast so that your souls do not get corrupted."

Before he could continue, the server brought the food, and all three were so hungry that none of them muttered a sound till it was time for dessert.

CHAPTER 12

Zaraquel

She ate her dinner without speaking. Zaraquel heard what Uncle Mac had to say, but she was confused by his words. "Do you mean we should lie to the witch? How do you know she will help us to begin with? I'm scared."

Nimue held her hand and squeezed. "I am too, Z, but if we want to bring Rae back, we must. Remember what she told us. And then we must find the totems and other stuff. I will be with you. We will do this together. I know I am not Rae, but I can be your best friend too. This way, you will always have two best friends, not just one. And when Rae comes back, we will be the unstoppable trio. Imagine the things we could do together."

Zaraquel smiled and nodded. Looking Uncle Mac in the eye, she said, "Okay, we will find this dark witch. Let's just not tell Mom and Dad what we are doing. They may not like it."

McPherson nodded, though he muttered to the girls that Chloe might already have an idea. Zaraquel dismissed the words and was excited to be able to begin working on bringing Rae back. She needed Rae.

Going back to the SUV, Zaraquel settled in again and decided to read a book while Nimue played games on her phone. They continued the journey, and at one point, Zaraquel noticed that Uncle Mac was no longer driving. He used a spell to control the car, like autopilot, but it allowed him to sleep, though he looked awake so that no cops or anything would pull them over. It was neat that he knew all these spells. She figured it had to do with how old he was. He was an old guy... well, not really. But old enough, she thought.

Zaraquel started practicing some of the spells in the book she was reading. It was part of her studies with Uncle Mac. She was learning how to control the elements of weather and nature. Outside her window, she was able to see the spells both work and fail. But her determination eventually paid off when she mastered the chapter in the book regarding the subject. Deep down, she felt confident but didn't want to seem arrogant, and yet at the same time, she wondered what this witch would be like and what she would teach. She pulled out her phone and began searching the Internet for the witch's story. There was not much data to find, but somehow Zaraquel knew it might be in the library of the Order. She connected to the library's system and began reading on the witch. It was all there. As she continued to read, she could feel a tingle in her wings. She was not liking what she read, but she wasn't about to let Rae down.

Suddenly, she came across a chant with no explanation. Nothing in the text told her what the chant would do. Curious, she said the words out loud, and suddenly, it got eerily quiet. Thunder crashed, and a lightning strike hit the road. As it did, Zaraquel glanced up and saw that the noise woke McPherson, and he gripped the wheel tightly. Another lightning bolt hit the ground, and this time with the flash, the figure of a woman appeared in front of them.

McPherson screeched the brakes, and the SUV came to an immediate halt. Somehow, Zaraquel seemed fixated on the woman and stepped out of the SUV. She walked straight to the woman and repeated the chant she'd learned from the Order's library.

The woman used both hands and made some movements in the air at waist length, and from her fingertips, she sent a dark light that encompassed Zaraquel. Zaraquel could not move, but she managed to yell for McPherson. She could hear him running towards them.

"Stop, knight of the Order. It is this one who summoned me, and I came. What do you seek from me, child?"

McPherson stopped in his tracks from what Zaraquel could see from the corner of her eye.

"I seek you, mistress of the dark magic. It is you, isn't it? Are you not Anne Koldings, known as the mother of the devil?"

"That was the name given to me at my birth. But yes, I am the mother of the devil and many other things. What is it you want? You are a child of the light, are you not? I

am protected by the one that goes by the name of Sammael."
Zaraquel could see that the woman was eyeing her up and
down. "But yes, you call him the Tall Dark Man, as you refuse
to acknowledge his true name. I wonder why?"

"I don't call him anything, but yes, his name is
Sammael. And yes, I am a child of the light. I am an avenging
angel, an angel for justice. But I sense you already know that.
Don't you, witch?"

The woman laughed. "A truthful child. But I sense
there are secrets you hold. Perhaps I should discover those
secrets. Or will you tell me what you seek from me? Most
people today leave me alone, but you sought me out."

Zaraquel, remembering what Uncle Mac had told her,
decided to make her own destiny. Her own choices. "I need
a teacher of the dark magic. I must learn it to bring back Rae.
She was taken from me, and it is my duty, my oath, to bring
her back. But I will not become a dark witch. I must have
balance between the two to succeed. So, I called on you to ask
you to become my teacher. But I won't be the only student if
you say yes. There's Nimue too. She's in the car. So, will you
teach me what you know?"

The woman looked past Zaraquel and pointed her
crooked finger towards the car. Zaraquel spotted a strange-
looking birthmark on her wrist. She spoke from what she
remembered from Uncle Mac and the reading. "You wear
his mark. You are the strongest of all dark witches. You were
chosen by him, by Sammael."

Smiling at Zaraquel, the witch said, "I will teach you
and Nimue, but you are to come with me now."

Having heard this, McPherson began to protest.

"Silence again, or I will seal your mouth shut. If I am to teach them, they must come with me now. Return to this very spot when I call for you, knight of the Order. Do you hear me?"

McPherson nodded. Zaraquel was scared but excited at the same time. She spoke to McPherson through their minds.

We will be fine. This is the way it must be. I know that somehow. I can't explain it but come back for us, please.

McPherson said, "I will return when their lessons are done. But witch, hear me clearly. If you harm either child, I will call the wrath down on you, and even Sammael will not be able to save you."

Nimue came out of the SUV, also in what looked like a trance to Zaraquel. The witch snapped her fingers, and all their belongs appeared in front of Zaraquel on the road. The witch opened a portal, and all three of them walked through it, leaving McPherson alone on the road.

***

McPherson

McPherson sat in the SUV for the remainder of the night, leaning back in his seat. He knew what the spirit had told him, but he couldn't help but worry for the girls. This witch, she was hard to make out because she wouldn't even hold a conversation with him.

As he slept, the spirit visited him once more. *Wake up, knight. Your path is coming. Stay true to the course and let the pieces fall into place. You can't hold back the avenging angel, for she has a higher destiny than any of you realize. She was once born to be the scepter for the queen. Now, she must be reborn to hold the balance of all magic. Through her, the next prophecy can come to light. Everyone must play the part. She will be tested, as will you. You may face foes. You may have to face friends. But awake now, for your path is here.*

McPherson stirred but managed to open his eyes. Heavy with sleep, his eyes opened, and he woke to a strange light. Gathering up his pack, he left the SUV behind and followed the light. His legs did not tire—he knew he must have been walking for what seemed like hours—but as he glanced at his watch, he saw the time had stopped. Finally, the light stopped, and it appeared that his path just stopped cold. At least that was what he thought until he couldn't believe his eyes. He rubbed them, because he thought he was dreaming. He still saw it. He rubbed his eyes once more in disbelief, even closing them and reopening them. But there he stood. Well, there they stood. McPherson remembered the stories Michael and Marcus had told about Kabos and how he was a spirit. But there he was, with no other than Rowe himself.

"How...how can this be? Is it you, Rowe? I am speechless. But after tonight, I am not sure what I trust with my eyes anymore. Or am I going to die?"

The spirits laughed, and it was the figure that resembled Kabos that spoke.

"Dear boy, I haven't laughed so hard since I can't remember when. Rowe and I are keepers of the prophecy. In fact, there are several of us. When our purpose here has been fulfilled, we continue to serve the prophecy in another way. We were sent to guide you on your journey. I believe your charges are looking for certain artifacts, but they can only be obtained by either members of the Order or keepers of the prophecy. Shall we go?"

Rowe spoke. "I know I left you with a heavy burden, but it was one you could handle. The child, the angel, she has a greater purpose than any of us can realize. Amber is a great queen of all the races, but her destiny lay in the battle just fought. Now, the angel child, Zaraquel, must rise to her destiny with the help of the queen, her mother, the light witch, and her father, the vampire."

McPherson couldn't believe what he was hearing. Another destiny for one of these great friends. But deep down, he knew that the Tall Dark Man would never stop, even if he fell into the pit. He had that much nastiness in him to remain alive. But onward to find the totems.

CHAPTER 13

Zaraquel

Zaraquel knew the witch would somehow betray her, but she needed her as her teacher. On the other end of the portal lay a small dark cottage in the middle of what appeared to be nowhere. As she clasped Nimue's hand tightly, Zaraquel followed the witch. Looking around, she thought this was like one of those eery cabins in the woods where the ax murderer comes out looking for his victims. It gave Zaraquel the chills up and down.

"Put your things in that room over there and come outside. We begin now."

Both girls did as told and were outside in the darkness. There was no light anywhere except from the fire pit that lay before them.

The witch looked at them intently from what Zaraquel could figure out. She would either teach them or eat them.

As she gave Nimue a look that meant that both girls had the same thought, her wings could not be hidden any longer. They sprung out, and their crimson red color shone against the firelight.

"What is this? Child, you hold secrets you will share with me, or I will not teach you. I will abandon you as if you were never here."

Zaraquel looked down at the ground and spoke. "I am an avenging angel. But I need you. I would like you to be my teacher in the dark arts. Teach me so I can balance both the light and dark magic to save my friend Rae and bring her back. In return, I will offer you freedom from whatever binds you. I can do that, I think. I look to seek out justice, and from what I read about you, I don't know if it is true or legend. So tell me, Anne Koldings, mother of the devil, is your story true? Did you give birth to all the demons and things of the night that serve him?"

The witch replied, "No one calls me by my name given to me at birth anymore. I haven't heard the name Anne in hundreds of years. But yes, my story is true. I served Sammael then, and I serve him now. In return, I never lost my beauty or my age. He pulled me from the fire and gave me immortality in exchange for birthing his demons. I am one of the most powerful dark witches to walk the earth. More powerful than Elizabeth Hexham, more powerful than any other witch except my equal to the light. Chloe is her name, related to Sarah Good. But looking into your eyes, I see that you know her, child. In fact, there it is. You are her daughter. A daughter of the light, and now you want to be a daughter of the dark."

Taking another deep breath, Zaraquel nodded. "I will not lie to you, witch or Anne. What would you like us to call you?"

Nimue then added, "I like the name, Anne. I am willing to learn from you, and I also served him. But then I also was the apprentice to the one called Merlin. I know the ways of different magics, not just the dark arts or the light. But I know the ways of the Celtics, the ancient Druids, and many others. I am in this to help Zaraquel."

The witch looked at them again. "So, you too served Sammael. Is that so?"

Zaraquel wanted to learn so badly that she said, "Yes, but we call him by other names. He likes to fool you into thinking he is not one and the same, but he is. I feel a desire inside to learn dark magic. It is a pull that I can't explain. So will you teach us?"

The witch said it was time.

And she began to teach the girls the first and most basic spell of the dark arts. Zaraquel executed the spell masterfully while Nimue watched. She also tried and was successful.

"I think I would like it if you girls would call me Anne. It is a name I haven't heard in a while, and sometimes I do miss it. Now, watch and learn this next set. These are hexes and curses. Once you master these, then we will begin on casting spells to conjure demons and the like."

The rest of the night or day, whatever it was in this place, took a toll on Zaraquel, and somehow, she could sense the same for Nimue. But Anne kept up the teaching. Little by little, she could feel her light dimming, but she focused hard to keep it bright. Zaraquel continued to master the spells flawlessly, and before she knew it, Nimue became sluggish and quiet. Zaraquel spoke to Nimue through her mind.

Stay strong. Feed off my light. Remember, we can't be pulled into the dark magic, no matter what.

Nimue began to feed off Zaraquel, but not too much. Time passed, or it didn't. The girls had no way of knowing as everything stood still.

Finally, Anne let them rest. Zaraquel fell onto the bed, and not long after, Nimue followed. The routine became the same, day after day. Zaraquel lost track of the time, lost track of the days that surrounded her training. More spells, more magic, more demon possessing.

Finally, it became clear to Zaraquel that there was something else happening inside her with the training. But she couldn't make sense of what it was.

Until Anne decided it was time to learn necromancy. She remembered dabbling a little into it with Rae, out of curiosity, but it did not go far. Anne had Zaraquel and Nimue raise the dead, using the entrails of a corpse to control it as if they were brought back to life. The more Zaraquel learned necromancy, the more powerful she became in the dark arts, so much that she didn't see the tips of her wings changing as if they were dying. Zaraquel struggled with her morality, her sense of justice with each passing day. The lessons were easy for her to accomplish. And when she felt the need to practice light magic to keep the balance, Anne forbade it and made her go to bed without food. As far as Zaraquel was concerned, this was wrong.

"Something is wrong here. Anne, I thought you would teach me. But I feel different. I thought you and I were becoming friends, but something is wrong with me."

Anne gave her a sweet smile, but Zaraquel didn't fall for it. "Nothing is wrong. It seems you have a natural talent, a natural hunger to serve him. Can you feel the power growing inside you?"

"Yes...Yes, I can. I will resist it, wait and see. I love the power it gives me, but not like this."

Looking upward, Zaraquel closed her eyes and screamed. She didn't just scream. She called for her mother, the witch of light to find her, to save her. Her moral compass was in jeopardy, and judging by the look of Nimue, she was already back on the dark side.

"Mom, I need you. Follow my light. Save me."

Somewhere, somehow, her light broke through the darkness, and she hoped her light would be strong enough to lead her mother to her. As she waited, she collapsed on the earth where she could feel Anne levitate her body and bring her inside onto a table.

She knew Anne was hovering over her, chanting and calling out his name.

In her mind, she was saying *This can't be happening to me. No, I won't let it. Mom, where are you? Uncle Mac? Save me someone. Save me, please.*

Within moments, Zaraquel could hear Nimue scream. Nimue was fighting this dark power. She had the light in her still.

***

Nimue

Before Anne could finish the chant, Nimue gathered all her strength and called upon the most ancient of orders to help. She called upon the teachings of Merlin and the Druids of the earth. A blinding flash of light shone through the dark cottage and forced an explosion upon its structure.

"You will not sacrifice Z to him. Not now, not ever. We trusted you, witch. For that, I will kill you myself."

Suddenly, Nimue was standing next to another, and it wasn't Zaraquel. She couldn't tell who it was, but she was familiar enough. "Is that you, Chloe? Are you here?"

The shape smiled and said, "I am here, but only via projection. It is something I have mastered quite well if I can come to this dark place. Hold out your hands and point your inner palms at her. Repeat these words after me.

"Drink from my light but be cursed by my light.

Take my power from me but be cursed by my power.

Give Zaraquel your power, your last breath.

I break you from his curse and cause you to bleed."

Nimue did exactly that and watched as Anne fell to a heap on the floor, bleeding and eventually crumbling into the earth.

The shape of Chloe faced Nimue and began to speak. "Listen closely. I can't enter this dark witch's home in my flesh, only spirit. Find a spot in the earth and consecrate it. I know you know that spell. It is something the Order teaches all, and if you were a student of Merlin's at one point, then I trust he taught you as well. Consecrate the earth and bury

Zaraquel in it to heal. Marcus is coming for you both. The teaching is not done yet, but Marcus will stay and find you another teacher. She must not lose her soul to that witch."

Nimue found the safest spot and consecrated it. She buried Zaraquel into the sacred earth and waited for Marcus. She knew she had to tell Zaraquel that the journey was not yet done, and her moral compass lay in the balance of good and evil till...well, who knew for how long.

***

Zaraquel

Zaraquel lay buried on the ground, asleep in a trancelike state. She could not move, but her mind was active. She could hear Nimue whispering over her, begging her not to leave her all alone. Zaraquel couldn't put the pieces together of what had happened despite how hard she tried. She was learning the dark magic and was mastering all of it. Zaraquel also sensed she was losing herself somehow. She remembered how Uncle Mac taught her how dark witches can feed off a light switch, draining them of their light.

She heard Nimue again. She remembered. Was the witch dead or alive? Nimue said her life was hanging between the balance of good and evil. Rae told her to maintain the balance. She didn't know what to do. Her mind raced through all that had brought her to this state, unable to move, unable to communicate. Then a familiar voice entered her memory. Her mother. Chloe, the witch. But how? She must wake up from this dream.

Then she remembered what she heard. Forget

calling her Anne any longer. The witch's new nickname was "witch bitch" for doing this to her. Zaraquel called upon all her strength as the avenging angel, daughter of Chloe and Marcus, to free her from this. But her strength was bound by something dark. She couldn't use her light magic. Zaraquel then realized if she gave into the dark magic, she would lose herself. She let her body and mind relax, trusting in Nimue. She could hear everything that was happening.

The witch summoned her magic and called to the Tall Dark Man. "Lord and master, I summon you here, whether in spirit or flesh. I have the angel child, but you must hurry. She is in a consecrated ground, but if we free her quickly, we can link her soul to yours. I cannot be sure of the results considering her power, but it is worth a try. There isn't time to spare."

Zaraquel heard that and refused to let herself become his slave. Then she heard her dad calling their names. Zaraquel became alert, waiting. She heard him arguing with the witch and then something else. As she listened, Zaraquel realized he was tearing into her flesh. But it wouldn't be enough to kill the witch. Zaraquel loved her father, Marcus, but he was not that strong. She sensed what he was doing. He had drained the witch of some of her blood, but the blood touched the consecrated ground, and it was burning. The holy ground was burning the blood! But it was enough to send a jolt through Zaraquel's body, causing her wings to extend, and she pulled free from the earth, but not on her own accord. Her body floated up and glowed. She couldn't open her eyes; she couldn't move. But something was doing this to her. An unknown force of power. She prayed it wasn't the Tall Dark Man.

Moments had passed, and Zaraquel awoke, still floating in the air. Her arms rose, and from her back, she pulled out a sword — a sword that appeared when she needed it most. She pointed the sword towards the witch and spoke. "I am Zaraquel, Avenging Angel of Justice. I will master the balance between light and dark. I will wield the Sword of Justice, and I command you, witch, to unleash me, or I will seek my revenge upon you."

The witch cowered in front of her, saying, "I serve the master. I must do his bidding. He wants you on his side. He needs you, not the queen. Not the others. Since the last battle, he has a different plan. One that requires you, your soul, to be his demon warrior angel. I can't unbind you. Something inside of you won't let me unbind you. This was not my doing. This was your doing. Unbind your soul. Kill me if you must, but the master will only bring me back, for I cannot die, angel child."

Zaraquel almost dropped her sword upon hearing those words. Her soul was bound to something, but she didn't understand how she was doing this to herself. The witch must by lying.

"I don't believe you. Set me free."

The witch raised her hands and tried to show her she did not bind her, but something inside her unleashed. Zaraquel kept the sword pointed at her with one hand while the other unleashed a bolt of lightning. Marcus, somehow, leapt into the air and pushed her back so that a bolt of lightning wouldn't kill the witch, causing more unwanted surprises.

"Daddy, help me." As she fell to the ground again, she said nothing else.

***

Marcus

Marcus used his vampiric speed and overpowered the witch. He told Nimue to stand back and take care of Zaraquel.

"Witch, this time, you will meet your maker in Hell."

Grasping her hair, he pulled her head back and bit down on her. He didn't care if she lived or died. The witch screamed and begged him to let her go. He stopped drinking from her. As she gasped for air, she laughed and poked fun at him.

"You think he's going to let you just kill me? You are a fool. He gave me eternal life. All I must do is deliver this angel to him. I see you in her. She's your daughter. The master wants her at his side to punish the queen."

Controlling himself, he let out a few choice words for the witch. Nimue interrupted and said, "Zara called her the witch bitch. I can't understand why she didn't like it. It is what she is."

"Not now, Nimue. Focus on healing, Zaraquel."

Marcus took another bite from the witch. This time, he tore into her flesh and spit out the skin, leaving the artery exposed and blood spewing onto the earth. Then he smelt it. Her blood smelled of pure evil, pure darkness.

"Okay, witch bitch. My daughter needs a teacher. You are the darkest teacher she found. What will it cost you to train her but not turn her over to your master? I will stay if that's what it takes for her to learn, but you can't call your master here. In return, I will let you live in your so-called cottage, or what's left of it."

The witch thought long and hard and laughed at him. "I am the mother of the devil. There is another more powerful witch than I. The most powerful witches haven't birthed the master's demons. He has left her untouched, and she is of the Hexham witches."

Marcus, upon hearing that name, cringed. He remembered the Hexham witches too well. They destroyed Rae, who was like a daughter to him, and Zaraquel's best friend. Letting go of the witch, he stood over her while she cowered, laughing at him.

"Tell me of this other witch. I need one of you dark witches to teach my daughter. Tell me or suffer. I am not playing games with the likes of you."

The witch stared up at him. As she sneered, she refuted to him, "You won't be able to find her. She never leaves his side, not even to visit her family. Raven is the one you want, but she only does the master's bidding. Raven taught us all, though, and increased our power. If your daughter needs a teacher, I will do it. But I have to give the master something in return. What do you have that I can satisfy him with, vampire?"

Marcus had nothing to offer. He stepped away and talked to Nimue. He wanted to know if the girls had negotiable items. Nimue shook her head. Marcus returned to the witch and offered himself to the witch, but on his terms. The master could have his soul, his life, but Marcus chose the time. He reiterated his terms to the witch to ensure her understanding. Marcus would decide when and where he would surrender.

"Take it or leave it."

The witch spoke the terms out loud while she summoned the master. She replied to Marcus that the agreement was accepted. She also confirmed the master would wait for Marcus's terms to surrender his soul. Marcus thought, *Chloe, is going to kill me.*

Chapter 14

Nimue

Nimue watched the witch making a brew. She and Zaraquel were to practice the spells the witch was teaching them till they were perfect. These spells were like the ones Merlin had taught her but different. Merlin taught her to respect the magic and the universe. The witch was teaching them the opposite. She looked over towards her and noticed that Zaraquel seemed weak. Nimue offered to help her, and she was happy that Zaraquel accepted it.

The witch brought two mugs for the girls. It was a strange-smelling brew, and as much as she tried to be nice, Nimue didn't trust her. Because Zaraquel was still so weak, she took the brew and drank it. The witch was watching her as she sipped. Nimue continued to sip the brew. Each sip caused her to gag, leading to coughing.

"Drink it. What are you waiting for?"

"It's too hot."

Nimue shrugged and took the smallest sip she could muster. It tasted as gross as it smelled, but as she sipped it, something inside her kept telling her to resist it. She was hearing someone's voice calling to her.

Daughter of the lake. You were never abandoned. I am always with you. Remember what I taught you.... The rest faded, and she heard no more. The memories would come and go until she could decipher their meaning.

She wished McPherson was here. Where was he?

The witch said, "Finish the drink, little one. It will help you master the spells. Don't you trust me, little one?"

Nimue nodded. She continued to drink the brew while trying to monitor Zaraquel. Her friend didn't look well. But she needed to buy time while trying to figure how to escape. Zaraquel continued to drink the brew while Nimue continued to take small slips, sometimes even just pretending to let the liquid into her mouth. It was not easy to do, but Nimue was determined to save her friend.

***

McPherson

McPherson walked through the forest with no set direction. He followed the clues the spirits would show him, and yet he still wandered. When they appeared, he enjoyed his long talks with them. Seeing and talking to Kabos might help him understand the prophecy and those he loved. It was good to see Rowe again. He could learn how Kabos and the prophecy were connected. Before anything, he told Rowe about leaving Nimue and Zaraquel with a powerful dark witch, and something inside him told him things were not quite right. He figured it was instinct.

Rowe looked like he was deep in thought. "Let me see if I can remember how to communicate with Nimue. I'm a ghost now, so things might be a little tricky."

As Rowe was silent, McPherson moved closer to Kabos.

"Kabos, tell me more about Michael. Before he became Michael. His death, and his becoming Machiel, tore at us. Especially Amber."

Kabos laughed and started telling him all about Michael. The stubbornness, the women, everything. Kabos spoke of the stone that Michael found when he was Machiel. It was a turning point in the young man's life. McPherson now understood why he may have been easy to corrupt. He was not just a vampire; he was a conduit for evil. Because he walked away from the prophecy for a journey, his soul was open for evil. There was more. Michael, just like Amber, was also a conduit for past atrocities. The prophecy had these two in mind. McPherson was piecing certain things together. He understood Amber would need to be stronger, better, and more cunning than ever before to succeed. McPherson was curious about the book even more.

Kabos explained the book was his responsibility because of his mother's bloodline. In order to fulfill his destiny, Kabos had to become a vampire. McPherson listened and even asked questions that led to Kabos holding his hand up. "The Tall Dark Man can't take Michael's stone. Upon Michael's death, the book and the stone will choose a new master. The new master would have to give the stone to him willingly with their blood."

"I understand. But what is this book?"

"Ah, yes, the book. The book is about the prophecy. This book will choose its master, and only death can sever that bond. The master can read the book and, of course, the true gypsies, but no one else will understand its language. Michael and I never finished reading the book because it only reveals the parts that the master needs. Marcus does not know about this book. We couldn't risk many people knowing about it. We didn't pay too much attention to the past, as we were concerned about the upcoming battle.

"But I digress. The book talked about a first battle. It happened starting at creation. The world would face its first battle. The second battle was not the last. The Tall Dark One, in the book, is noted as the master of a dark prophecy. The one prophecy we have to prevent. He had four stones that were sent with servants to protect before the upcoming battle and to keep safe until they were needed. These stones were destroyed except the one Michael received. It is with the book on his estate. Children of the gypsies were taught that the master destroyed the stones and his servants. All but one stone. The Stone of the Damned. Misfortune brought Michael to that stone. Long story short, the stone became part of him, bending him to the will of the master. He broke free with the help of friends, the Dire Wolves. Michael learned to control the stone, though it weakened the purity of his heart. This made him vulnerable to revert to Machiel. The stone and the book are in the estate, hidden. Remember that the Stone of the

Damned is tied to the book. Marcus knows nothing about it."

McPherson took a moment to digest what he learned before answering. He understood. He asked Kabos to continue, but he insisted that while they were spirits, his human legs needed to rest. They did while Kabos continued his story. McPherson saw Rowe was still lost in thought, so he might be communicating with Nimue.

Rowe finally said, "It didn't work, but I will keep trying. Keep going, my friend. I will always catch up if I need to, but I need to keep at this. Something was blocking me from reaching Nimue, but I know what I must do."

Kabos spoke. "The first battle was called the Battle of the Beginning. There is a fifth stone known as the Stone of the Forsaken. It destroyed the other stones, the master's servants, and the wolf line. The other races suffered through numbers, but it was the wolves that were endangered. We could never understand why. The master was furious and vowed revenge on us all. That stone remains in his possession. The book speaks about a third and final battle involving that stone. This is the ultimate blood prophecy. Michael's stone, when combined with the fifth stone, could open a portal that will unleash evil into the world. No amount of light and goodness will stop it. What is unleashed should frighten us all. The world as we know it will be nothing more than a ravaged land where the most vile creatures of darkness roam free, and we are the hunted. The balance would tip to the dark and evil side, where the Tall Dark Man will reign as king. The most recent battle was to prepare Amber and the angel child for their ultimate fight. To prepare for this final battle, the races combined their powers and created certain totems. You're looking for the symbols of life and death. This is what the angel child needs in order to maintain balance. To prevent the annihilation of all."

***

Zaraquel

Zaraquel was reeling from the prior events and figured her strength hadn't fully returned. She looked at the cup, gave a small smile, and drank. To her, this was a tasty drink, but as she watched Nimue, she couldn't understand why she wasn't drinking it. *Maybe there is something wrong with it? I must lean on Nimue until I am stronger. My head is so fuzzy.*

She looked at the witch, Anne, and thought she was nice. Each time she performed one of the dark spells, a little part of her light would fade. She asked her what was happening.

"Anne, I don't get it. Something is wrong. I can feel it. I do what you say, and I conjure these dark spells, but something inside me is fading. It's like my heart is breaking with each spell. My light is fading. How can I balance this? I need to, except I don't feel well."

The witch touched her hair, and Zaraquel noticed her hair was changing, becoming darker and coarse. Zaraquel ran her fingers through her hair, hoping to get the witch to stop, to no avail. Zaraquel was feeling lost, and she wanted her mother to come to find her.

"Child, drink the brew. What is happening is what happens when anyone of light magic touches the dark magic.

Don't you trust me?"

Before she answered, Nimue did. "NO! We don't trust you. You serve the Tall Dark Man. You only agreed to teach us because her father said he would surrender himself to him. You are a witchy bitch. We don't need her, Zaraquel. We can find someone else to teach us and save Rae. And we can save your dad. We don't need her. She's doing something to you. Can't you see?"

Zaraquel couldn't believe what she heard. "M...my father. He surrendered himself? Why?"

The witch told her it was to save her and have her learn the dark magic. Something had to be given to the master, and he offered himself. He was valuable to the master.

Zaraquel screamed at the top of her lungs, and before anyone could respond, her wings spread, and a strong black aura seemed to form around her, but then it was mixed with a bright light aura. The light aura tried to shine through over the black. Zaraquel noticed it, but the light wasn't strong to penetrate the blackness.

Nimue said, "Z, you're glowing in both light and dark."

The witch said, "Child, you are making progress. I kept my word. I am teaching you. I had to dim your light in order for you to accept the dark magic. One will consume the other and change you if you don't balance it. I serve the master, but I kept my word. The brew has done its job for now. As for Nimue, you already had the dark magic inside you. It's the light magic you need to learn. I cannot teach you that. You need a light witch."

Zaraquel was confused, but she understood. Closing her eyes really tight and curling up her little nose, she tried to find the strength inside her to make the auras equal. She clenched her fists, but it just wouldn't happen. She thought, *Soon I will balance this.*

***

The Witch

She watched the two girls closely, particularly Zaraquel. She had never seen such power in a young woman. The master's instructions were clear. She was to teach them the darkest of all magic, hoping the angel would lose her light quickly. As she watched the young woman, she became so entranced by her gifts that she lost sight of the master's intentions. He wanted the angel, but the reasons were unknown to her. Zaraquel was a quick study, beautiful and quite spunky for a young adult. Looking at her closely as the days passed, she knew Zaraquel was losing her light, though she only told her it was dimming. This was all part of the plan. Her master was brilliant and intent on his revenge.

"Zaraquel, let me teach you this spell. You too, Nimue. Come closer, girls."

The girls made their way towards her, but Zaraquel insisted on getting a notepad first. The witch nodded and pulled up the chairs. Nimue sat down, and they waited for Zaraquel to return. The witch talked about the spell of Undoing. As she spoke to them, she noticed that the girls' faces were intrigued, yet they looked a little frightened. Softening her tone, she explained the spell.

"The spell of Undoing is the darkest spell a witch can learn. Undoing refers to separating your soul from your body or the person you are casting the spell on and connecting it to the master's soul. You would have to be in his presence to complete the spell. The beginning can be done anywhere. Shall we get started?"

The witch set up a table covered with a black tablecloth, and black candles adorned it. In the center sat a framed picture of a goat.

"Zaraquel, I need you to stay focused on the picture. Look straight into his eyes." The girl nodded, and the witch seemed pleased with her obedience. "Now, you do the same, Nimue." Nimue also gave her a nod.

Clasping her hands together, the witch began the chant.
"On this black day;
I release thy soul;
Bound to you;
I now become whole;
Undo thy will;
Call me unto you."

"Can you girls remember those words? Go ahead, write them down if you need to. It is important to memorize these spells. Now for the next part. It can be said in advance by four hours. If you wait longer, the spell will not work. That is the second important piece if you start the spell in advance. The spell of Undoing is not complicated to say, but the timing makes it an advanced level spell."

The girls were staring directly into the picture, safe for the moment because they were not saying the chant. This allowed the spell not to work. As she watched them more, she decided it was time to continue.

"Before we continue, the spell isn't working because I said the chant. In order to cast the spell, you must say the chant. Okay, the next part. You must prick your finger and spill one drop of blood onto the master's cheek. Or the person who you are doing the spell with to connect your soul to theirs. Try to prick your fingers now."

The girls pricked their fingers and allowed one drop of blood to fall from their fingers onto the floor. The witch was pleased and smiled, noticing the aura around Zaraquel was becoming darker. She told them the next spell would be the spell of control. Tomorrow's lesson. The witch released them from their studies, which made them happy to just relax.

CHAPTER 15

Zaraquel

Zaraquel was practicing with Nimue when she sensed her dark magic becoming stronger than her light magic. In fact, she tried to spread her wings, and once she did, she noticed they didn't open as easily as before. In fact, their beautiful red color was fading. She didn't reach the next level of justified kills, so that couldn't be the reason. Could it be the effect of the dark magic on her? She wondered if she was being reckless by staying with Anne, the witch, and not leaving as Nimue had urged her. She remembered the deal her father made for her to seek this teacher. Inside, her heart felt heavy and broken.

She practiced another spell, one that the witch taught her specifically, and tried it against a tree. Nimue interrupted and told her she sensed Zaraquel was losing herself. Nimue was begging her to stop. She couldn't.

"Z, please stop. We can't continue. Something is wrong even if you don't believe me. Look at your wings!"

Zaraquel was feeling the power of the dark magic and liked it. Her eyes narrowed in on Nimue, and before she knew it, she called upon the dark power and tried to cast spells on Nimue to disable her. The spells that McPherson had taught both girls before were blocked by Nimue. The girls continued their magical battle, and Zaraquel collapsed to the ground. Her wings were almost a full dark gray, not a good sign for her as an avenging angel.

"My wings! What is happening to me? Nimue, I'm scared."

Nimue crawled to her, and Zaraquel noticed how much she was struggling. She realized she had just defeated her friend. Tears flowed down her cheeks but stopped as soon as Nimue reached her. Her hand reached out towards Zaraquel, and their fingers almost touched before Nimue collapsed again.

"Nimue, come back to me. Don't leave me. I didn't mean to hurt you. I need you. You are becoming like a sister to me."

Zaraquel inched herself with all her strength to be close to Nimue, to touch her. The minute their fingertips touched, a blue ball of light encompassed both girls. They were floating in this ball of something, but Zaraquel didn't care. Nimue wasn't moving, and her eyes were closed. Was she dead? Did she kill another friend?

Tears flowed and reached Nimue. Nothing happened. She didn't wake. As she continued to cry, Nimue remained still, unmoving. But the flowing of the tears changed her wings back to red, slowly, but they were still mostly gray. But there was enough red in them to keep her balanced. Zaraquel began singing a song she remembered from her mother. Nimue moved once more. Her eyes slowly opened, and Zaraquel grabbed her friend in a hug as they continued to float in this blue ball of light.

Nimue was alive again! Zaraquel vowed to find the balance and not let the dark magic consume her.

"I don't know what it is. It just happened when we touched fingertips, and I cried. Nimue, what did I do?"

Nimue shook her head. She said she'd heard about it. "The ball is energy or balance. It is what keeps us whole. I think Merlin said it is light and dark in the world. I know a little more. I'm still weak, Z. I'm so tired. But Z, you must stay true. Don't let the darkness consume you, or he will win." Her eyes closed once more.

Zaraquel took it upon herself to call every bit of light magic she had in her. She breathed deeply as if she was in a meditative state. Her wings turned a little more red. The blue light that encompassed them disappeared, and she found them on the earth once more.

***

McPherson

He continued his journey with his spirit-like companions, Rowe and Kabos. He learned a lot more on this journey than from a book about the totems. Kabos finished telling him about Michael and even mentioned how he blamed himself for failing Michael. McPherson reassured him he was never at fault. He felt he understood Michael more now than when he was alive. He was guilty of not knowing what was happening to his friend.

Rowe and Kabos stopped. McPherson kept walking but noticed he was walking alone. He realized that the two spirits were not moving. Heading back to where they stopped, he surveyed the ground, the trees, everything. Nothing stood out to him. Then he felt it. A light cool breeze, which seemed odd for the dark forest. He used the magic from the earth to get a sense of anything that may have caused Kabos and Rowe to stop dead in their tracks. He tried to speak to them, but they remained silent. Unmoving. It gave him the most eerie feeling of all.

Making a cup with his left hand, he placed his right hand over it about six inches apart and moved his right hand counterclockwise. A red light was created and stayed within his hands, forming a ball of magic.

"From the earth, I seek thee,
From the earth, my ears hear thee,
Speak to me, dirt of earth, sands of time,
Show me what I must see."

Out of the corner of his eye, near some trees, he saw a faint light. Walking toward it, McPherson saw another light. Every time he moved, lights appeared, and as he figured it out, he realized the lights made the shape of a pentagram. There was a large hole. McPherson was both curious and afraid. He looked down into the hole. He glanced back at Kabos and Rowe, who remained still and quiet for spirits.

He went to where they were standing and tried to communicate with Rowe. Rowe was powerful. This shouldn't have been complicated. After all, he was Merlin. He tried different spells on Rowe to get him to respond, to no avail. He peered down at the hole. After all, he'd asked the earth to show him. He couldn't see anything but darkness. Reaching into the hole, he felt nothing on the earth. He didn't understand why there was nothing.

He thought long and hard about this. Pulling a dagger from his pants pocket, he gripped the handle and cut into his left palm. He let his red blood trickle into the earth and chanted a different spell.

> "With my blood, I bind my life to the earth,
> I open my eyes to see.
> I open my ears to hear,
> My life I bind to the earth,
> My soul I bear to the earth."

The earth trembled with the drops of his blood. The leaves from the trees moved in the wind, and the air became thick. McPherson continued to breathe, though it was hard. He felt his blood merging with the soil. This forest must be older than anyone could realize. His body could feel what the earth had felt for centuries. The battles, the spills of blood, the birth of nations. Everything. And then he saw it. A vision. What he saw could not be unseen. It terrified him, and, in his heart, he called to the earth to show him the totems, if possible, but he'd be humbled with anything the earth would have to show him. The earth responded.

A totem flew up from the hole and landed in his hand. His blood mixed into the wood of the totem and caused the totem to glow once before darkening. He looked at the totem and noticed its pagan like design that represented death. The blood was now infused into the totem, allowing him to hold it. He knew what the Totem of Death meant. The keeper of the totem would be granted the power of necromancy, something that went against his beliefs. Therefore, he wrapped it in a cloth and tucked it in his pack.

Once the totem was covered, Kabos and Rowe were freed from the momentary stillness. McPherson cracked a smile at them and started laughing before he told them they were still as statues for quite some time. He then continued to tell the two of them how everyone was doing, and that Rowe nodded and said, "Of course. It makes sense now. But that means we are getting closer to finding the next one. It is as I have foreseen a long time ago. We must hurry. Let's go. I will try to reach Nimue again."

***

Nimue

Nimue and Zaraquel returned to the cottage after practicing their dark magic, barely speaking to one another, only to find the witch cooking something. As they entered through the door, Nimue had a bad feeling. The witch wasn't waiting for them like she usually did. Zaraquel flopped on her bed and looked exhausted. She noticed that Zaraquel's wings were not fully red like before, but at least they were not fully grey either. This might be a good sign.

She felt sick from the last power blast from Zaraquel. Her stamina hadn't returned yet, but that was the least of her concerns. She felt a little off balance. She felt the good light magic returning—the magic she was born with from her days with Merlin. Before she became dark. The feeling made her happy. But it didn't take away the pain she felt for her friend. She let Zaraquel rest on the bed while she gathered her strength to see if she could eavesdrop on the witch bitch. Zaraquel's nickname for the witch was growing on her. It even brought a smile to her face.

Easing around the corner, she glimpsed the witch, making a kind of foul-smelling soup. Then she noticed it, laying on the counter—mandrake root. A sudden pain almost caused her to scream, but she bit her hand to keep from making a sound. She was curious about what the witch was cooking. As she continued to watch, the pain in her head wasn't letting up. Then she recognized it from a very long time ago. She forced herself to listen. It was Merlin. He was communicating with her. How could this be? He was gone. Or he wasn't. The pain was real.

Merlin was trying to tell her something. This time, he wasn't yelling at her for her callous ways. He was pleading with her to keep Zaraquel safe and that he understood everything now. Was it really him? Asking her for help? She wasn't sure, though Merlin never lied to her. She listened to him and followed his directions that he gave her.

Nimue, I have always forgiven you. Do not forget that. You must save Zaraquel at all costs. Only a true friend can help her now. You are that friend. Save Zaraquel to save us all. Follow my instructions carefully. I need to see what the witch is doing. McPherson filled us in about her teaching you, and this is a very dangerous road you both are on. After you show me, I need you to find McPherson. He is not alone. We are with him, but time is of the essence. He needs your help to find the remaining totem. The totem of Life. Hurry!

She projected herself to move about the cottage in a cloaking spell and got closer to the witch. She watched the witch add the different ingredients into the pot while the mandrake root lay on the counter. It was moving. She thought she could hear it cry. It was so fresh.

The witch said, "Once I control the angel, the master will be pleased. He might grant me favor in his coven. I must plan for Nimue's accident. The angel must not have her allies or friends with her. Time to let this simmer. Once it is ready, the 'darling' angel will be in a deep sleep that only the master can awake her from. She must turn to the darkness."

That was all Nimue needed to hear, and she ceased the spell. She hoped this spell gave Merlin what he needed, as she had allowed him to see through her eyes. She was his conduit. She also realized that the witch planned to double-cross them and go against the deal she made with Marcus.

Fearing she would be discovered, Nimue returned to Zaraquel and placed her hand on her forehead. Her friend must survive on her own for a while. Nimue needed to find McPherson, even if she had to break her promise to Marcus. She knew McPherson could help them after he found the totems. She didn't want to break that promise, but she knew she had to. With her hand on Zaraquel's forehead, she whispered her message to her friend.

"I will return for you, but you must be strong against the witch. I must help McPherson find the totem, or you can't bring back Rae. My friend, my sister, stay strong."

And with that, she chanted a protection spell over Zaraquel that she hoped would keep her friend safe until she returned. Grabbing her bag, she slipped out the window and made her way out of the woods. It was difficult with the barrier spells, but Merlin helped her along the way. She hoped that by leaving Zaraquel alone, she would not lose her moral compass because if she did, then Nimue would have failed.

***

Nimue

Nimue made her escape from the witch's cottage and was able to use all her power to break through from the shield that kept them hidden. Not knowing where she was only proved to be more difficult. Tired and weak, she needed to rest for a bit. She found an area that would provide her cover and sanctuary while she slept. Nimue asked the land to provide her aid, and in return, she would honor the land when she could return the favor. She had little magic left to finish this spell and oath.

It must've been hours before she finally regained her strength and started searching for McPherson. She used another spell, taught to her by Merlin, to find where someone was. Luckily, she had secretly put something in her pack that belonged to McPherson. Nimue pulled it out and conjured a spell to bring her directly to him. She remembered what Merlin had said. There was no time to waste. She wandered through the forest clearing and stumbled a few times.

"McPherson! McPherson! It's me, Nimue. Where are you?"

She continued to walk through the forest and noticed how dark it had gotten. The forest was changing before her eyes. It grew darker and darker. Finally, she spotted McPherson and some other shapes. Nimue shouted louder, and he must've heard her now because once he turned around, he bolted towards her and embraced her in the biggest hug she had received in a very long time.

She was a little out of breath when he let go. Nimue said, "I came as quickly as I could. I got Merlin's message. Where is the totem?"

McPherson handed her a wrapped item and told her it was the Totem of Death. She felt it in her hands without removing the cloth and closed her eyes. Saying a spell while one hand moved slowly above the object, she announced, "The Totem of Life is nearby. The two are in close proximity to each other. Where is Merlin?"

McPherson looked at her, and she couldn't quite make out his facial expressions. Then he pointed to one of the shadow like figures behind him. Nimue saw Merlin's figure and smiled. Running to him, she fell to her knees and bowed her head in shame.

"Forgive me, teacher and friend. Once, we were lovers, friends, and enemies. I seek redemption for the wrong I caused you."

Merlin smiled and told her he went by the name Rowe now. He was just happy to see her safe and away from the Tall Dark Man.

The group, together, called to the forest to show the path to the Totem of Life. The forest began to change once more as Nimue made her way deeper into the center. The trees began to appear livelier than they ever had before. Nimue closed her eyes once more and laid down on the earth. She was next to the largest tree, and with an extended arm, she touched the tree. No spell was needed. Nimue just connected herself with the tree, using the power of the Lady of the Lake. From the tree, a crevice opened, and a young branch moved towards her hand and laid the Totem of Life in her palm. She opened her eyes and blessed the tree.

Smiling at McPherson, she handed him the totem. He looked at it and nodded, but he didn't take it. Instead, she wrapped it alongside its mate. The balance of life and death. Nimue knew that Zaraquel was headed on a dark path with the witch. She only hoped she would get there in time to save her and her moral compass.

I was born in Hawaii, a place rich with culture and storytellers. As a little girl, scary tales about vampires, werewolves, angels, demons, and witches were my favorite kind — much to my mother's dismay.

The scarier, the better.

My love for the supernatural never went away, even after moving to Seattle, far from Hawaii's majestic beaches with unusual colors. Nothing compares to the landscapes of Maui, Lanai, or Oahu. But somehow, Seattle stole my heart anyway. It became the place where my love for stories took on a new form in a book of my own: The Adventures of Little Arthur and Merlin the Magnificent. This book is for kids who love stories, just like I did.

Then I had an idea while sleeping.

One night, my mind began to work overtime. In a dream, I saw a unique storyline involving all the races and an epic battle of good versus evil. It was a modern-day plot with a three thousand year old prophecy, The Blood Prophecy. I finished the first book in 2014, The Queen's Destiny. Two years later, I released The Queen's Enemy. The last book in the series, The Queen's Ascension, arrives this Spring 2020.

Today, I live in Florida with its beaches and sunshine. But I'm still a Seattle girl at heart. And so, all my stories take place in the Northwest.

I always keep to my roots when I write.

- Barb Jones